Divine

Tarot

True Colors
Natural Evil

Thea Harrison

Divine Tarot
Copyright © 2013 by Teddy Harrison LLC
ISBN 10: 0989972844
ISBN 13: 978-0-9899728-4-0

Cover Design © Angela Waters

Print Edition 1.0

Original publication in ebook format by Samhain Publishing:
True Colors, 2011
Natural Evil, 2012

True Colors

Dedication

To Heather and Amy, and my family for
making this possible.

Chapter One

Death

Don't move. Stay perfectly still.

The enormous monster plunged through the apartment with the lethal speed of a stealth bomber. A Molotov cocktail of pheromones and Power spewed through the blood-tainted air, the classic signs of a strong male Wyr in a rage. Alice clung to her perch, her heart knocking so hard she thought it was going to burst out of her chest. Had the murderer returned?

Then the monster slowed. Alice heard him utter vicious curses under his breath as he came upon Haley's still-warm body. Alice took the New York subway daily to work, and thought she had heard it all, but she learned a few things as she listened to him. Did he curse because he saw the murdered woman for the first time, or because he realized he had made some kind of mistake?

Alice had only just arrived at Haley's apartment herself. She had found the door open and rushed inside to discover that her friend's body had been laid out on her bed. Haley's torso had been cut open, organs lying across the flowered bedspread like a child's abandoned toys.

Alice had gone numb at the sight, the normal cool, gentle logic of her mind seizing in shock. Then she had heard someone running up the stairs. She had barely gotten to her hiding place before the monster appeared. If he was the murderer and he had returned to clean up some clue he had left behind, neither Alice nor the police would know what it was now.

He prowled through Haley's home in complete silence. Alice couldn't even hear the soft pad of footsteps. Her awareness of him was excruciating, as though someone had stroked the flat of a razor blade along her bare skin with the smiling promise of a cut. His presence was a violation of Haley's private space. He paused not two feet away from Alice, so close she could see the pocket of his worn leather jacket out of the corner of her eye and hear the almost imperceptible sound of his steady breathing.

She wanted to scream and strike at him. She wanted to run away and dial 9-1-1. The shadowed apartment hallway was a million miles long, the open front door too far away for her to make a run for it and hope she wouldn't be noticed. She didn't dare move, did not dare even shift her gaze for fear a glancing light might reflect off her eyes and give her position away. She hardly dared to breathe. The only thing she could do was taste the air and know that, if nothing else, she could recognize this man again by his scent. Underneath the scent of violence, he smelled warm and clean. If they were in any other kind of situation, she would have found his scent sexy. She fought the sudden urge to vomit.

Wait. If she could scent him, then what kind of trail had she left behind? Could he scent her as well? Would he be able to recognize her again, too? *Oh gods.*

Riehl struggled with his rage and got it under control. His body settled out of the partial shapeshift. He couldn't shake the feeling that someone was watching him. He kept one hand close to his holstered SIG P226, and an invisible six-pack of whoop-ass ready in the other.

Dead body with the same M.O., evisceration of the abdominal cavity. The killer never took the organs. He only set them out in a distinct pattern, like stars in a dark constellation. The average human body held 10 pints of blood. This woman's once-pretty bedspread was drenched with hers. It dripped onto the carpeted bedroom floor in a thick, heavy pool. He wouldn't be surprised if it had already soaked through the floor to the apartment below. Someone was going to have a bitch of a time cleaning that out.

Goddammit, the body was still warm. Her keys and half-opened purse were on the floor, and the ruins of a business outfit pillowed her mutilated body. It looked like the killer had surprised her as she arrived home from work. There was no sign of forced entry, which meant she had thought she had reason to trust him. Had the killer posed as a utility or maintenance worker, or was he an acquaintance?

If Riehl didn't find anybody else to open the whoop-ass on, he could always save it for himself. If he had made the connections a little faster, if he had heard back from the Jacksonville PD a little sooner, if he had run the internet database searches right away instead of jawing over ideas with his new boss, Wyr sentinel and gryphon Bayne, this pretty lady might still be alive.

Goddammit, this was partly his fault.

He needed to call HQ, but... Riehl did a slow swivel, his sharp eyes noting every detail of the place. The vic's home was a tiny, postage stamp-sized one-bedroom on the top floor of a four-story walk-up. It was furnished with space-saving IKEA décor. To Riehl, the vic had kept the apartment so warm it felt stifling. A flat screen TV was mounted on one wall. Every small-apartment dweller in New York must have cheered when that innovation came out. There were plants and books and shit, such as a tangle of female frippery on a bedroom dresser. He nudged closets open and they were full of normal stuff—clothes, shoes, coats and a few umbrellas, and small boxes. A Thursday paper was folded on a Barbie doll-sized dinette table, alongside an open box of holiday decorations with an elegant feathered and sequined half-mask perched on top.

Christians had Christmas, Jews had Hanukkah, and the universal African holiday celebration was Kwanzaa. For the Elder Races, winter solstice was the time to celebrate the seven Primal Powers in the Masque of the Gods. The vic had been in the middle of decorating her home for next week's Festival of the Masque. Maybe she had planned on attending one of the many balls that were held throughout the city. The mask was a nice one, the kind one wore and passed down to one's kids. It had set someone back a paycheck or two. Maybe she had looked at it with happy memories and anticipation.

All in all, the apartment was pretty typical for the city, and a perfectly charming place for a petite, 135-pound single female like the vic. Riehl stood six-foot-five and topped 263. He had only recently decided to domesticate himself from ninety-six roaming years spent as a captain in the Wyr lord Dragos Cuelebre's army. He was used to a rugged lifestyle and spending a lot of time outdoors, often in inclement weather. To him the small overheated place felt claustrophobic.

There was no doubt in his mind the killing itself was the reason for the invasion. Her jewelry still lay scattered on the dresser and the corner of a wallet was visible in her open purse. It looked like nothing had been taken, unless the killer had snipped off a little something from one of the organs to keep as a souvenir, which would have to be determined by an autopsy.

He just couldn't shake the sense of someone else being present. He was looking for some kind of fricking giveaway. Someone's eye peering out from behind a closet door, or a webcam stuffed in a cute pink bunny. He even scoped the snow-covered scene outside the window to see if someone was watching from another building.

As he searched he took in deep, even, deliberate breaths. The heavy copper scent of blood pervaded everything. It all but buried the vic's normal scent. There were other odors that he classified as normal and dismissed, like the faint lingering scent of fried fish and some floral stink that came from a bowl of potpourri. If Riehl had been in his Wyr form, his wolf would have had a sneezing fit at the potpourri and looked for the fish to roll in.

He noted two other very interesting things. He could taste faintly at the back of his throat a chemical tinge that hung in the air around the vic, along with the smell of rubber. He would bet his next week's paycheck that the killer had worn rubber gloves, and that the chemical taint was *KO Odorless Odor Eliminator*, handy tool of deer hunters and Wyr criminals everywhere.

He would have expected the gloves, but using the KO meant the killer was either Wyr himself or at least he was familiar with Wyr investigative capabilities. The killer was organized, knew how to hide his scent, and planned ahead. That all fit with the deliberate care with which he had set out the victim's organs, which was an exact match with the Jacksonville slaughter from seven years ago.

The second, very interesting thing Riehl noticed was another scent in the apartment. It was a light, delicate, feminine scent that tantalized his senses. Haunting and delectable, it hinted at an unforeseen, mysterious reality he wanted to dive into headfirst, except that the scent had turned jagged with stress pheromones that set his teeth on edge and had his hand inching closer to his weapon. The scent hadn't had time to sink very deeply into the surroundings and was already fading.

The body was still warm, and a woman had been in the apartment before him. Well, how about that.

If the stubborn prickle at the back of Riehl's neck was anything to go by, the woman might even still be around, although if she was, he didn't have the first clue where she could be hiding.

He came to a sudden decision and strode out of the apartment.

Last week's snowfall had turned to dark sludge in the streets and on the sidewalks, but the chill, wet December wind brought the promise of more. Fluffy flakes of white were just beginning to drift down. They looked innocuous and fairy-tale pretty, but they were the precursor of a major winter storm that would smother the city by the early morning hours. Snowplows had already begun working the streets. The wind tasted of exhaust fumes, fried food, salt and grit.

Riehl did a fast recon when he hit the street. No sign of a lingering perp, but then he didn't expect anything else. Dude might be killer whack-job nuts but he was not stupid. Riehl was not going to get that lucky tonight.

The dead woman's apartment was located in the melting pot of North Brooklyn, where a variety of Elder Races mingled with an ethnic hodgepodge of humanity. The gray smear of early evening was dotted with bright holiday decorations in storefront windows. The nearby street corner had a delicatessen/grocery store that was run by a Wyr family. They were some kind of grazing animal that liked to cluster in groups. The grocery store was across the street from a liquor store run by an older Armenian couple. The open-air newsstand had the strong earthy scent of a dwarf lingering around the edges of the door and hatch.

The newsstand had already closed for the day, and so had a dry cleaner's half a block away. The dry cleaner's shadowed doorway was far too shallow a nook to hide his broad-shouldered physique. Actually there weren't any good hiding places where he could hope to watch the apartment building and remain undisturbed.

Riehl moved fast, dodging vehicles to reach the delicatessen. He thrust through the doors and stopped in front of the cashier station by the street window. The cashier was a lanky, middle-aged male who gave him a nervous smile that vanished as Riehl pulled out his badge and showed it to the guy.

"Ignore me," Riehl said. The male nodded, his eyes wide.

Riehl went to the edge of the plate-glass window and flattened himself against the wall. At that angle he was hidden from the apartment building entrance. He tilted his head until he could see the front door. Then he waited. Riehl made people nervous at the best of times and if a woman had been hiding in the apartment, she was going to be skittish.

He considered. Could she have witnessed the murder? Even participated? The Jacksonville PD records made no mention of a possible partner. Had they missed something, or could it be a recent development? Would a killer that ritualistic make such a drastic change in his methodology?

Nah, he was trying to put too many curlicues on the whole scenario. If the woman had been an active participant, she would have been gloved and her identifying scent cloaked, and she probably would have left with the killer. And if she had witnessed the murder, she would have had plenty of time to escape the scene before Riehl arrived. And what sort of person could remain still and silent while watching someone get butchered with such precision? Riehl's already black mood darkened further.

As he watched, he pulled out his cell and hit speed dial.

Bayne answered. "Yeah."

"He got her," Riehl said. "It's our boy and the body's still warm. She couldn't have been dead more than an hour, hour and a half." He listened to the sentinel swearing.

Bayne asked, "What do you think, is it the Jacksonville killer or a copycat?"

"If you're asking me to guess, I'd say yeah, it's the Jacksonville killer. You have to eyeball for yourself the meticulous butchery he did here. A guy like that could have the self-control to wait seven years, if the wait had some kind of special meaning for him." He gave Bayne the address and said, "Listen, I gotta go. I'm following up on a possible witness."

"I'm heading over to the scene myself. Call me back when you can," Bayne said. The sentinel disconnected without saying goodbye.

Riehl started to pocket his cell just as the apartment building door opened and a woman stepped outside.

He froze. Everything froze. Body, mind, spirit. The world tilted on its axis and repolarized.

Though the woman's torso was hidden in a thigh-length black woolen coat, it was clear she had a slender, elegant frame. An abundance of gold-tipped, dark brown corkscrew curls sprang out from her head. She wore straight-cut jeans, boots, and wire-rim glasses, and her complexion was the rich, warm color of cocoa and cream. She carried herself with the tense fragility of someone suffering from deep shock. Even from across the street, her thin intelligent face looked strained. She reached the sidewalk and paused, one narrow, fine-boned hand holding the high collar of her coat together in a defensive gesture as she scanned the street.

It was her, the woman from the apartment. He knew it. He didn't have to catch her scent. Horror and tragedy still lingered in her eyes.

Another kind of knowing settled into his bones, a strange, deep pool of certainty that he had undergone an undefined, irrevocable shift that he didn't understand or have the time to explore. The woman turned and began to walk in the direction of the nearby subway station. Riehl pushed through the delicatessen door and moved to cross the street, the whole of his attention laser-locked on her retreating figure.

✧   ✧   ✧

Alice's feet started carrying her automatically on her normal route home after visiting Haley, toward the Bedford Avenue subway station. First Peter was killed. Then yesterday they found out David had gone missing, and now Haley was dead.

David was dead as well. She knew he was, even though the police had not yet released any official word. Three of her friends, gone in as many days.

The street looked innocuous but a hint of the monster's scent still lingered, warm and sensual in the cold wet air. Alice couldn't stop shaking. The image of Haley's poor mutilated body was frozen in her mind. What was she supposed to do next? Oh yes, call 9-1-1.

She dug in her pocket for her cell phone as her gaze darted around her surroundings. She glanced over her shoulder.

A man in black jeans and a battered leather jacket was crossing the street. He was immense, as tall as a tree, built like a linebacker, and he moved like a killer. His white-blond hair was cut military short, and the sharp, ruthless lines of his face were weathered and harsh. His piercing eyes were some kind of pale color, either gray or blue, and they reflected the light as he looked straight at her.

The bottom dropped out of Alice's world as recognition slammed into her. Too many nightmarish epiphanies happened at once. They nearly knocked her to the ground.

It was the monster. He was no longer caught in a Wyr's partial shapeshift, but she knew him. She *knew* him.

He'd found her, just as she'd been afraid he would. He had caught her scent, and now he had seen her face.

And she had seen his. He might be the one who had killed her friends. He was the most terrifying male she had ever seen.

And he was her mate.

Oh gods. Oh gods.

A hot wash of horror licked invisible flames along her skin. She had heard of such a thing before, two Wyr recognizing each other as mates at first sight. She had thought it was an urban legend. Deeper than love, more dangerous than lust, Wyr mated for life. This couldn't be happening. It wouldn't happen, not if she had anything to say about it.

She whirled. Terror whited out her thinking and lent wings to her feet.

Riehl lunged into a sprint after the woman.

Holy hell, that chick could move. Riehl was fast but he was big. She darted lickety-split between cars and people like nothing he'd ever seen, her slight, slender body able to take sharp turns and squeeze through tight spaces in a way he couldn't hope to match.

Then in a hopscotch skip straight into the land of weird, as she ran she faded into her surroundings. She didn't quite disappear, not totally. Her clothing was too solid for that, but somehow it was harder to track her just by vision alone.

Huh. That was fascinating as shit.

Good thing he could track her with more than just his vision. He could catch her if he changed. If they had been anywhere but the city, he would have. He was faster in his wolf form, and he could run literally for days. But if he changed into the wolf, he couldn't speak unless they were close enough for telepathy, and he could already taste her panic on the wind. Besides, NYC might be the seat of the Wyr demesne, but it was also home to millions of others as well. He didn't trust how people might react to the sight of a two-hundred-pound wolf hurtling down a city street.

He took a deep breath and bellowed, "NYPD! Stop!"

Of course she didn't stop. He wouldn't have stopped either just because some dumbass stranger yelled at him. Damn it, was she headed for the subway?

She was. In a move that was so suicidal it took his breath away, she plunged almost directly under the wheels of an oncoming truck as she raced across the street. Riehl didn't think the driver even saw her because the truck never slowed.

Riehl had no choice but to pull up for a few vital moments, which gave her an even greater lead. After the truck he kicked it in gear, kicked it as hard as he could. He blazed down the sidewalk like a heat-seeking missile, scattering pedestrians in his wake like so many squawking chickens. He listened to the sounds of his breathing, the sharp wind whistling in his ears. At the subway station, he didn't bother with taking the stairs at a run. Instead he gathered himself and spanned the flight in one massive leap, but it wasn't enough.

Several yards ahead, the woman darted across the station platform and on to a train just as the doors closed. It was like something out of a goddamn made-for-TV movie. Unbelievable. Riehl spat out a curse as he came up to the closed doors.

They stared at each other through the barrier. The woman was panting and her eyes were dilated black in a face that was chalky white except for two hectic flags of color in her cheeks. As she took in his expression, she stepped back from the door, only stopping when she bumped into people behind her.

The train lurched. He raised his eyebrows, pulled out his badge and showed it to her. She stared at it and her eyes widened. As the train pulled away, she stepped forward again and put her hand to the glass, her gaze rising to his.

He pointed to her. "Nearest police station," he mouthed. "Go there."

The last sight he had of her was her peering at him as the train rattled away. He wondered if showing her the badge would get a better result than yelling at her in the street had.

He had better go locate the nearest police station and find out.

Chapter Two

Law

A lice got off the subway at the next stop and ran up the stairs to street level. She was a total wreck, spooking at the slightest thing while she tried to think past the incredulous shout still echoing in her head.

Had he experienced the same epiphany when he looked at her?

Mate. Killer.

Police?

Be smart, be safe now. Could the badge have been fake? Rattled though she was, that seemed like an awfully unlikely stretch—unless impersonating a police officer was how he had gotten inside Haley's apartment in the first place. Haley's door had been open, not broken. Many crimes had been committed by people posing as police officers, including one of the most famous in the twentieth century, the St. Valentine's Day massacre in the 1920s.

But he'd told her to go to the nearest police station. That sounded authentic—unless he hoped to grab her before she actually got inside. Why would he do that?

Now she was sounding paranoid and irrational—except she had left the normal boundaries of reality behind two days ago when she heard that Peter had been killed.

Their group was small and tight-knit for a reason. The shock waves of Peter's death had barely begun to reverberate through the circle when Alex Schaffer, the group's leader, had emailed everyone yesterday to tell them he couldn't get in touch with David and had anybody else heard from him?

Nobody had. Alice and Haley had planned that very evening to huddle together and grieve for Peter and fret over David's disappearance. Alice had been ready to coax Haley into packing a bag and coming to stay with her for at least the weekend, and not fifteen minutes ago she had realized that the dark red hollow at the midsection of Haley's sprawled body was in fact the inside of Haley's body.

If that man was the killer and he had come back to Haley's apartment to clean up something, if he thought she could identify him and tie him to the crime, he would want to do anything he could, even risk proximity to the police station, in order to get rid of her.

She ran into a small piece of luck as a taxi drove down the street with its light on. She waved at it and when it stopped, she jumped in and locked the doors. "Drive around," she told the cabby.

"Okay," said the cabby. He was an intelligent, anemic-looking Wyr in his mid-forties, with a dry, dusty scent and fingernails bitten to the quick. He glanced over his shoulder at her. "Anywhere in particular you want to go?"

"I'll tell you in a minute," she said. "Just get moving."

"Fabulous," the cabby said with a shrug. "It's your dime."

Alice pulled out her cell phone and finally dialed 9-1-1. For a wonder, an operator picked up after only a few rings. "I need to report a murder," Alice said.

The cab slowed, and her driver gave her a sudden sharp look in the rearview mirror. She glared at him and he ducked his head. The cab picked up speed again.

The snowfall had thickened. Alice watched the passing streets through the windshield wipers while she gave the operator Haley's address, and what details she knew. "When I left the building, a man chased me," she said. "He had been in the apartment. I managed to get on to a subway train as the doors closed so I got away from him, but he had time to show me a badge through the window. He said he was a police officer and he ordered me to go to the nearest station. I need to verify his identity if I can."

"Ma'am, I can't do that for you over the phone," said the operator. "You need to go to the nearest police station."

"Look, I'm a teacher," Alice said. Her voice unraveled along with her composure. "I'm not some tough soldier or cop-type that deals with crime scenes and death every day—I teach first-grade kids, okay? Usually the worst part of my day is trying to get the glue and glitter off my jeans after craft-time and preparing for parent-teacher conferences. Now I've had three friends killed in the last three days. Today it was one of my best friends, and her body is in pieces. I'm shaken and I'm really scared. What if this man's waiting for me outside the station and he's not actually the police?"

"All right," said the operator, her voice gentling. "Here's what we're going to do. You said you're in a cab, correct?"

"Yes," she said.

"Have your driver pull over and give me your location. I'm going to get a unit dispatched to you. Make sure you wait in the cab with the driver until they arrive. Then you'll have a police escort to the station. Okay?"

Alice's world stopped spinning just a little. She whispered, "Yes, okay."

Less than ten minutes later, a cruiser pulled up behind the cab, lights flashing, but siren off. Alice paid the cab driver as one of the officers, a policewoman, walked up to them. Alice climbed out of the cab.

The policewoman said, "Alice Clark?"

"Yes," Alice said.

"I'm Sergeant Rizzo. My partner is Officer Garcia. We're here to escort you to the 94th Precinct."

"Thank you," Alice said. She had cooled down after her headlong run through the streets, but her clothes were still clammy with sweat and the temperature was plummeting fast. The winter storm had definitely arrived.

She wrapped her coat tight around her as she started to shiver.

"You're welcome." The policewoman walked with her to the cruiser.

"I'm sorry to trouble you," Alice said. "I don't even know if this was necessary."

"Not at all," said Rizzo. The Sergeant opened the back door and gestured for her to climb in. "From what I understand, you might have been facing a smart, violent killer. You can't be too careful."

As Alice settled gingerly into the backseat, Garcia twisted around to smile at her through the protective grille. "We've got a message for you that might set your mind at ease. We just heard from the WDVC—the Wyr Division of Violent Crime. Detective Gideon Riehl has arrived at the 94th and is waiting for you there. He says to tell you he's big and blond, and he's sorry he scared you."

Alice sagged as Garcia's words sank in. "Oh gods, thank you."

Reaction set in as Garcia drove through the thickening storm. Alice huddled in her coat and shook so hard she felt like she might fly apart at the joints. A succession of images from the past hour flashed through her mind with silent urgency.

Haley's expression had been blank, as if she had died overcome with surprise. Or perhaps her expression was blank only because she was dead, and she had suffered unimaginable fear and pain in her last moments. Had she looked into her killer's face and known she was going to die?

Had she looked into her killer's face and known him?

Alice wiped her face with the end of her scarf. Haley worked—had worked—at the same elementary school as she did. Someone was going to have to call Alex, who was not only the leader of their group but the principal of Broadway Elementary. Someone was going to have to contact Haley's parents. She supposed the police had an established protocol for such things, but Haley was—had been—an only child. The news of her loss was going to be a crippling blow. Maybe the police would let Alice help.

And Peter. They hadn't released the details of his death, only that he had been attacked and killed. They might not have found David yet. But as early as two days ago, when Alice and Haley had talked of Peter in hushed voices in the teacher's lounge, Alice had known.

The nightmare had returned.

Though the Friday evening was still young, traffic had thinned to a trickle as visibility was reduced to yards. A winter storm advisory urged emergency travel only and even the most determined holiday shoppers abandoned their pursuits.

The world had turned barren and so treacherous it leached away the electric welcome of lights shining in the dark. The wind howled as though it was populated with invisible wolves on the hunt. It drove the snow with such force tiny needles of ice attacked any exposed skin.

There were two kinds of storms, Alice thought. One was a friendly kind that you could enjoy watching out the window with a cup of tea. It crashed around in the sky with theatricality but no real malice.

This storm was the other, the killing kind. There are horrors that exist in the night, the bitter wind said, horrors that only children and demons can see. There are horrors that exist in the mind as well, that only the individual can bear witness to. The winter wind sang of things that the mind did not quite remember but that fear never forgot, filled as people are with the haunts and tragedies that make up the shadows of their lives. We can't endure them, the wind whispered, for when the light and warmth are truly taken we are left shivering naked in the dark. Then we hear a nearby husky chuckle that tells us we are prey.

Not even the lights of the 94th Precinct could offer Alice any comfort as the square brick-and-stone building appeared suddenly, a great, hulking, shadowed mass in the gray-and-black night. Faceless evil destroyed her friends and stalked her community. The grief and fear were crushing.

Then there was this, a different kind of reason to shake, an impossible sense of *knowing* about someone she didn't know at all. The conviction invaded her bones and assaulted her skeptical, resisting soul.

She didn't want a mate. She didn't even like to date. All of those questions everybody asked, the same ones, over and over. What do you do for a living? What do you do for fun? What do you like to eat? Are you seeing anybody else?

Did anybody ever answer those questions truthfully on the first date?

Alice's tendencies followed her shy Wyr nature. She was a quiet person who liked solitary pursuits. She enjoyed reading, quilting, long walks and biking in parks, camping and books on tape. Her idea of going renegade was to make a radical departure from a food recipe. While she adored all fifteen of the quirky, rambunctious children in her classroom, she often spent her evenings at home recovering from the intense social interactions of the day. She got her social needs met by the routine get-togethers of her group, other teachers at lunch, periodic phone calls and letters to her parents and, oh gods, *Haley.*

The gigantic menacing stranger—what had Garcia called him? Detective Gideon Riehl. He couldn't be who she thought he was. She had to be suffering from some kind of internal system malfunction, a strange by-product from all the stress of the last few days.

Wyr were deadly when they turned criminal. By definition, anyone who worked in the New York Police Department's elite WDVC lived a violent, dangerous life. In order to bring down criminal Wyr, the members of the WDVC had to be better, more efficient killers than the Wyr they hunted. Alice couldn't imagine anyone more unlike her. No wonder he had terrified her.

Had he felt something when he'd first laid eyes on her? Did he share the same, insane conviction that she was his mate? If he hadn't, she had to worry about herself. If he had, then she had a whole lot of other things to worry about.

She caught sight of Detective Riehl's unmistakable, immense figure as he paced in front of the precinct's doors. He was bare-headed, his battered leather jacket unzipped. Apparently he was immune to the brutal blizzard shrieking around him. Riehl turned as Garcia pulled the patrol car over to the curb. He was already striding forward as the cruiser slowed to a smooth stop.

A powerful insanity took over Alice as she watched him approach. He moved his massive body with athletic, sure fluidity, those impossibly long legs of his making short work of the distance between them. His light-colored gaze fixed on her with the same unnerving intensity as earlier, but instead of filling her with panic, this time she knew that he was her only shelter from the killing storm.

Her gaze clung to him, her breath sawing in her throat as she groped for a handle, only belatedly remembering there weren't handles in the back of a police car when Riehl reached out and gently opened the door for her. His icy gaze steady, he held out both powerful hands to her.

Maybe she meant to run. The part of her that continued to be appalled wanted to. The greater part of her, the insane part, reached for his outstretched hands with both of hers. His palms were hot and calloused under her fingers. He supported her weight as she somehow got her trembling muscles to work and climbed out of the car. Her teeth were audibly clacking, her pride nowhere to be found. He gave her face one keen, searching glance then he simply enfolded her in his arms. His warmth and scent surrounded her, and the relief and comfort were indescribable.

"Everything's going to be all right now," he rumbled quietly in her ear. "You're safe. I've got you."

She gave up all thought of running, abandoned every sense of pride and propriety, and leaned against his broad, muscled chest. It felt like a strong and sturdy home.

Now that they were up close and personal, Riehl found Alice Clark such a wee little thing, he could almost pick her up and put her in his pocket. He rubbed her slender back as she huddled against him. For some reason his heart had decided to do a jackhammer tempo. The wolf in him growled as she trembled, but he kept a stern hold on his beast. Now was not the time to go all Cujo on anybody and run the risk of freaking her out even further. But he angled his head and bared his teeth in silent warning as the two uniforms stepped out of the police car and approached a little too close.

The male uniform held up his hands in a placating gesture. The female narrowed her eyes on him and said deliberately, "Ms. Clark, do you need anything else from us?"

Riehl's snarl deepened as Alice's arms fell away from his waist. She would have turned away from him too except he refused to let her go. She turned her head instead. Her wild, adorable, gold-tipped corkscrew curls tickled his chin, and he wanted to rub his face all over her as she said, "No. Thank you for everything."

"You're welcome," said the female. She gave him an extra glare before turning away with her partner as they went back to their shift.

Alice tilted her head to look up at him. He assessed her strained expression. Thin, gold, wire-rim glasses framed large hazel eyes, brilliant with flecks of blue and green, against cocoa-and-cream skin so lustrous it made his mouth water with the urge to lick her everywhere. Her delicate, somewhat ascetic features were smudged with tearstains and lingering traces of fear. Standing out in the frigid cold, her shivering had increased.

Those beautiful eyes of hers were stark with too much emotion and remembered horror. He came to another one of his quick decisions and told her, "I'm taking you home."

Surprise bloomed like an unfurling flower in her tense, closed-down face. She asked, "You're not going to question me?"

"Yes, but you've been through one hell of a shock. Anything we have to say to each other can be done in the comfort of your own place," he said.

He put an arm around her shoulders and steered her toward his vehicle, a black, unmarked, late-model Jeep Cherokee. She didn't protest but moved at his side like an automaton. He unlocked the doors with the key fob and opened the passenger door for her. Once she was settled, he moved swiftly around to the driver's side.

With a quick sidelong glance, he made sure she had fastened her seat belt before starting the Jeep and pulling out. He could feel through the steering wheel how treacherously slick the road had become. The engine was still warm, so he turned the heater on full blast for her. If he had been by himself, he wouldn't have bothered. In most instances, he generated enough body heat for his own comfort.

Riehl had come to realize just how used he had gotten to roughing it since he had taken the new job. A recruit at age twenty, he had been in the army for longer than most human life spans. His wolf was still not comfortable with the decision to retire. Whenever he was in compact living quarters like the vic's—like Haley Moore's place—he often felt as if he might knock things over if he moved too quickly.

In fact, these last several months he had been entertaining serious doubts about his decision to leave army life and settle in the city. He hadn't been sure he could make the adjustment. The wolf had been satisfied with a roaming lifestyle, and the army had given him the sense of pack that he needed. It was the man who had gotten restless and decided it was time to make a change, but the restlessness hadn't subsided when he had relocated and changed jobs.

In fact, it hadn't subsided until just now.

He sent another thoughtful sidelong glance at his passenger. The storm was really dumping it outside, and white snowflakes had caught in her hair. They were melting in the warmth of the car. The remaining moisture sparkled on her like a net of tiny jewels. The line of her profile was sad, even stern, her delicate mouth straight and unsmiling. She was grieving, and he was the hind end of a donkey because he couldn't stop staring at her, and all he could think about was what it might take for him to get her naked.

He felt it again, the shift of the world's axis, the conviction that true north had moved and nothing would ever be the same again.

He felt it. He just had no idea what it meant.

The drive to her apartment should have been a short one but the weather made it much longer. Alice glanced at Riehl a few times when he took the correct route without asking. Her hands tightened as she clasped them together in her lap but she remained silent. He hadn't had time to do much when dispatch had contacted him, but he'd done a quick search on her name. Alice Clark, age thirty-five. Hell, he'd been in the army for longer than she'd been alive, for over twice her lifetime. DMV records stated she owned a Prius. He wondered if, like a lot of city dwellers who were car owners, she was a weekend driver.

Her address turned out to be a garden apartment in a brownstone near Prospect Park. After they parked, he followed her down the shallow, ice-slick steps to her front door. The decorative wrought iron security grille on the front window was coated in ice. Heat blasted him in the face as they stepped inside. He was already stripping off his jacket as she locked and bolted the front door.

Her pretty hazel gaze rose to his face and skittered away as her hands moved to unfasten the buttons of her black wool coat. Christ almighty, watching her disrobe even that small amount hit him like a mule kick. He sucked air and pivoted away to stare at the wall.

"If you don't mind," she said, "I would like to change into some dry clothes." She sounded breathless, her voice barely over a whisper, and it was so sexy it was as if she had run a finger lightly down his bare spine.

He shuddered, made a herculean effort and managed to articulate a few words. "You do that."

She switched on every light as she left. In her absence the room seemed too empty. As Riehl waited, he prowled through her living room and stood in the doorway to peer into the kitchen/dining area. The apartment was too hot, of course, but he knew it would be. Alice's home was larger than Haley Moore's apartment. It looked like it might actually have two bedrooms, and there was a back door. The spacious room was decorated with a few colorful sunflowers strategically placed to accent sage green cabinets. A stacked washer and dryer sat in an alcove that could be hidden by a wooden folding door cover. A sturdy, plain oak table with four chairs sat in the dining area.

He moved to look out the back door's window, noting with approval that it was covered with a security grille as well. What he could see through the storm's white-out was a small back garden surrounded by a privacy fence, now shadowed and covered with a thick blanket of snow. That tiny piece of real estate would be a refreshing haven in the spring, summer and fall.

So she didn't flaunt it, but she had more money than her friend. She could afford a bigger place with a garden, and to keep a car in the city.

Riehl moved back into the living room. Plain, comfortable furniture in earth tones, a couch, a rocker and one of those long chair thingies—what were they called? A chaise lounge. Lots of bookcases filled with a variety of hardcover books and paperbacks, potted plants all over the place, truly beautiful handmade quilts folded and laid along the backs of the couch and chairs, and in one corner another half-finished quilt was in a round hoop set in a floor stand. Several pieces of original artwork hung on the walls, lush jungle scenes filled with rich greens and the occasional spray of exotic flowers. Riehl wasn't, by any stretch of the imagination, an art aficionado, but they all had a similar style and seemed to be from the same artist. A glass-paned gas fireplace was set against one wall.

Alice had used the dimensions of the room well to create an oasis. It looked comfortable while also conveying a sense of space, brightness and a touch of outdoors. He turned on the gas fireplace and stood back. Strategically placed area lamps helped to create a quieter evening mood. With the flickering gas flames, he could almost imagine lounging at a fire ring outside surrounded by living greenery. Both wolf and man heartily approved.

Gentle sparks of her Power dotted the home, more like soft glows than anything else. The place smelled like her, that delicate, evocative, tantalizing scent. He took deep breaths and felt the tension between his shoulder blades ease. Her place was attractive and welcoming, but not fussy or pretentious. He didn't feel claustrophobic here. He felt good.

He heard her moving around in her bedroom and imagined her taking the rest of her clothes off. Instantly his cock hardened and strained against the confines of his zipper.

He was such a guy. Could he get more reprehensible?

She'd just had one of the worst days a body could have, and it wasn't over yet because, much as he wanted to let her rest and recover, Riehl was going to have to question her. He should be thinking about what he could do to help her out, not how she would taste, how she would feel writhing under him as he drove into her elegant body.

Speaking of what he could do to help. He moved to the kitchen. A tea kettle sat on a gas stove. He filled it with water and set the burner to high, then opened and shut cabinets until he found her tea supplies. That was where he got lost—she had so many weird teas he had no idea what to pick out. They were sitting in her cupboard, so she had to like all of them, right? He grabbed a box at random and prepared a mug, and when the kettle emitted a piercing whistle, he poured boiling water into it.

He knew the moment she stepped into the doorway to watch him, but he made himself take his time as he turned to look at her. She wore soft gray flannel pants, a loose, blue cable-knit sweater with the edge of an old white t-shirt peeking at the neckline, and house slippers. He was glad to see she had decided to get comfortable and knew he had made the right decision to bring her home. She looked calmer but still so sad, it wrung at his old battle-hardened heart.

He said, his voice gruff, "You were so chilled, I put the fire on and thought you might like something hot to drink."

She glanced at the mug and the kettle warming on the stove, and her expression softened into a gentle gratitude of such sweetness, it slipped past every cynical barrier he had ever constructed to keep the world separate from himself.

"Thank you," she said.

He gave her a curt nod as he fought to keep his feet in a world that had gone reeling.

The world had tilted on its axis.

And she was his true north.

Chapter Three

Hearth

Alice stared at the powerfully built man in her kitchen and fought the urge to twist her fingers together. His face was marked with rough lines and stamped with an edged maturity that could, from one moment to the next, turn dangerous. There was no softness anywhere in his features. They showed he had gone to many places and seen unimaginable things, and faced them all with intelligent, competent composure, and he didn't know what it meant to give up.

His presence spiced the air with exoticism and turned her familiar surroundings strange. She had thought her peaceful two-bedroom apartment was spacious, but somehow he filled the entire place up with his strong male energy. It bathed her tired senses with vitality and a renewed sense of purpose.

He had worn just a faded black t-shirt under the leather jacket. The cotton stretched taut at the bulging biceps and deltoids in his upper arms, and strained across the heavy width of his pectorals. He wore a gun in a shoulder holster. Her gaze snagged on it. For long moments she couldn't look away from the weapon.

As she had left her bedroom, she had noted with disconcertment that he certainly knew how to make himself at home without being invited. He had turned on the fireplace and was making tea.

Then he had looked up at her, and his icy blue gaze speared right through her. She would have said it was impossible, but that frighteningly ruthless face of his gentled, and she felt all her insides turn to mush. When he told her the fire and the tea were for her, it was the last thing in the world she expected to hear him say. She had to press her lips together hard to keep her mouth from quivering.

"Are you feeling better?" he asked. "More comfortable, at least?"

The sound of his deep, rough-and-tumble voice rubbed along her skin. The tiny hairs along her arms rose. She nodded wordlessly.

He continued. "Where do you want to sit, in the living room in front of the fire, or at your table?"

Still wordless, she indicated the dining table. He carried the mug over, set it on the table and held a chair out for her. She eased gingerly into it as she asked, "You're not having any?"

He gave her a sideways glance that revealed a hint of roguish charm so potent it hit her point-blank between the eyes. "I'm not a tea drinker."

Devastated at the intensity of her reaction to him, she swiveled her gaze downward in the direction of the mug and blinked at it blindly. She wrapped cold fingers around its welcome warmth and cleared her throat. "I have beer and soft drinks in the fridge, if you'd like something to drink."

"I'm good for now, thanks." He took the chair opposite hers and leaned his elbows on the table. He said quietly, "You do realize I've got to ask you some tough questions now, don't you?"

She nodded. "Ask me anything you need to, Detective."

"Hey." He ducked his head, trying to catch her gaze, and she let him. He gave her a quick, coaxing smile. "Please call me Gideon."

A small sliver of warmth worked its way into her constricted heart. She managed a small, brief smile back. "And I'm Alice."

"Alice, I'm not going to make any secret about this—I'm very glad to meet you, but I'm sorry it had to be under such terrible circumstances. I'm sorry about the loss of your friend," Gideon said, holding her gaze with his own pale blue eyes. They had seemed so icy not that long ago. Now they were filled with grave compassion. A dark understanding lay at the back of the expression. Alice thought, *he knows what it's like to lose people close to him.*

"Friends," she whispered.

"Friends," he amended. "I wish you hadn't had to see Haley that way. I would have protected you from that if I could have."

Somehow he said the exact right things. His simple words acknowledged his awareness that something lay between them, but the condolences placed the emphasis on what they needed to focus on at the moment. It steadied her as nothing else could have done. "Thank you," she said, sitting straighter in her chair.

"I want you to tell me everything that's happened to you over the last couple of days," Gideon said. "Take your time, and don't worry about whether you think it's important or not. I'll decide if it is."

"Everything?" She regarded him in puzzlement. "You're not going to ask me questions?"

"You mean like in a TV show, where the cops get what they need to know in three or four minutes of directed dialogue?" Warmth touched her cheeks and she lifted one shoulder sheepishly. He gave her a faint smile. "I'll ask questions later. Right now, I don't want to lead you or impose my agenda or opinions on you. There's always the possibility that you know more than you think you do, and things that I can't know to ask about yet."

"Okay." She sipped her tea to take a moment and collect her thoughts. Not half an hour ago she had been a terrified, all but incoherent wreck. Now she was certainly grieving, but she felt calmer, supported, no longer alone and vulnerable in the dark.

She felt safe.

She thought back a few days ago to how different life had been when she had gone blithely to work without a clue what horrors the week would hold. "I'm a teacher," she said. "I work at a private elementary school, Broadway Elementary. Haley worked at the same school. The principal, Alex Schaffer, is a friend of ours. At lunchtime he came to tell us that a mutual friend of ours, Peter Brunswick, was dead."

At first the words came slow and halting. Then they sped up and came fast and hard. Gideon remained a silent listener, his steady gaze and strong, sure presence a lifeline she could hold on to when she hit the rough bits.

She cried. She didn't want to but she couldn't help it. When she reached the point where she had looked on Haley's poor, violated body for the first time, she took off her glasses and covered her eyes with one hand as tears streaked down her face.

Gideon's chair scraped the floor. He came around the table, knelt beside her and pulled her into his arms. It felt like it had the first time, a sense of not just being hugged but enfolded.

Neither one of them remarked on the fact that, as a police officer questioning a potential witness, many people would say his actions were inappropriate. He had crossed that line already outside the precinct.

Alice gave herself a gift—she let herself do what she needed to. She wrapped her arms around him, tucked her face into his sturdy neck, and sobbed her heart out.

He rubbed her back and held her with immaculate patience, only loosening his hold when she had calmed and made as if to straighten. He asked in a quiet voice, "Better?"

She nodded and touched the back of his hand in thanks. Then she collected her glasses and stood to splash her face off at the kitchen sink. The cool water felt good against her over-hot, puffy skin. She patted her face dry on a towel and slipped her glasses back on her nose. As the world came back into focus, she noticed the clock built into her stove read 9:05 PM.

She looked at Gideon who had risen to his feet. Every time she laid eyes on him, the sheer size of him came as shock. Neither of them had had any chance to get supper that evening. He hadn't even started to ask her questions, so he wouldn't be leaving any time soon. She didn't think she could handle food, but large male Wyr, especially those with his kind of intense physicality, needed to eat.

"Are you hungry?" she asked.

He froze. She could tell he was trying to decide what would be the right thing to say and, unbelievably on such a horrible night, her lips curved into a real smile.

"Of course you're hungry," she said. "I'll fix something to eat."

"You don't have to do that," Gideon told her.

"I know, but I want to," she replied. "I like to cook when I'm stressed." His eyebrows rose. She chuckled a little. "I guess that might sound strange, but cooking calms me down. I find it comforting."

"As long as you're sure," he said cautiously. "I could eat something."

Given the care with which he was treating her, no doubt that meant he was famished, so whatever she made would have to be hearty. She was glad she had gone to the store to stock up on supplies when she heard the forecast for the winter storm.

She opened the fridge, pulled out a Corona and handed it to him. He took it, his eyes lit with a tentative gratitude. Good heavens, he looked like nobody had offered to feed him before. She turned back to assess the contents of her fridge as she tried to decide what to make. "You're a canine of some sort, aren't you?" she murmured. He would want a lot of protein.

"I'm a wolf," he said.

She paused as she absorbed that. A wolf, not a dog, which meant he was not quite tame or domesticated. Yes, that fit. He would be breathtaking as a wolf if his fur was the same white-blond as his hair.

"And you're a rainbow chameleon, right?" he asked.

The handle of the fridge door slipped out of her nerveless fingers. The door swung wide as she turned to face him and backed against a counter.

Gideon's expression changed. He said in a calm voice, "Alice, it's all right. Remember, you're quite safe."

Again, he played it to perfection. He didn't physically advance but instead leaned back against the dining table, his massive body relaxed, one foot kicked over the other. He regarded her with the same steady calm he had shown her all evening.

She relaxed with a self-conscious laugh. "I'm sorry," she said. "That felt like it came out of nowhere, and—we don't like to talk about ourselves or advertise what kind of Wyr we are, you know. Some of that's instinctive behavior, and some of it's… Well…" She made an all-encompassing gesture.

He nodded and rubbed the back of his head, looking thoughtful. "History has not been kind to the chameleon Wyr."

Like most of the Elder Races, Wyrkind were not only from earth. Some of the stranger species were native to the Other lands, those magic-filled places that had been formed when time and space buckled at the earth's formation. Rainbow chameleons were such Wyr. Rare, shy creatures, they came from a remote Other land connected to the Amazon rainforest.

Rainbow chameleons had no non-Wyr counterpart. They were also unique among other, mundane species of chameleons that typically could make only a few changes in color. Rainbow chameleons had the ability to change into any color and could do so at will to blend into their surroundings.

One of the earliest explorers of the Amazon inland, Spanish conquistador Francisco de Orellana, made the first known European contact with rainbow chameleon Wyr in early 1542 as he traveled the length of the Amazon River and searched for the mythical city of El Dorado. Upon discovering the rainbow chameleon's unique ability to undergo radical and complex changes in color, Orellana proceeded to commit some of the greatest atrocities in either Spanish or Elder Races history. He systematically hunted chameleon Wyr and had them dissected in an attempt to discover the source of their ability. The exact number of Wyr he murdered was unknown, but historians estimated the total to be anywhere from 3,000 to as many as 5,000, which were catastrophic numbers for such a rare species.

In his experiments, Orellana discovered the chameleon Wyr had a gland similar to the human pituitary gland. Extractions produced a fluid that, when it was used to treat textiles, could produce an arresting effect on items of clothing. Orellana never found El Dorado, but he brought vials of the chameleon extract back to Spain that he sold for a king's ransom while keeping secret its origins. Spanish royalty and a few certain wealthy nobles flaunted elaborate court attire made of fabulous cloths that changed colors with liquid fluidity to match their surroundings.

The secret of the chameleon extract was discovered in Orellana's papers after his death, whereupon King Carlos I and his mother, the mentally unstable Queen Joanna, outlawed the wearing of chameleon-dyed clothes upon pain of death. The Spanish monarchy made a great play at being morally outraged, but the political reality was, whatever their real reaction might have been, they had to make some gesture of public repudiation or run the risk of being destroyed by the infuriated rulers of the Elder Races.

However, rumors of the existence of such clothing had whispered through the succeeding centuries, in particular when connected to famous unsolved acts of theft. Whether those historical rumors were true or not, chameleon Wyr remained rare—Alice knew of only fifty or so currently living in the continental U.S.

The critically low numbers of chameleon Wyr made the crimes that had been committed seven years ago even more terrible. A small colony of chameleon Wyr had lived in Jacksonville, Florida, where seven of them had been found murdered the week before that December's Festival of the Masque. Despite a much-televised, nationwide manhunt by several cooperating agencies, the chameleon killer had never been caught.

The silence was broken by the wind that drove ice shards against the building, like a nightmare tapping the windows with skeletal fingers, looking for a way in.

Alice shuddered at the dark fancy and shoved it away. She was surrounded with light and warmth, about to be nourished with good food and drink, and she had been given the unforeseen gift of comfort and companionship during a time that would have been terrible to endure alone. She gave Gideon another apologetic glance and turned back to the open fridge to begin pulling things out at random. She said again, "We don't like to talk about our Wyr nature to outsiders. Does this have anything to do with our history?"

"You mean the conquistador massacre? We've found no evidence that links the present-day crimes to that." Gideon straightened suddenly. "That's how you hid from me, isn't it? In Haley's apartment. You changed into your Wyr form."

Alice looked over her shoulder at him, chagrined. "You knew I was there? You didn't just identify me by my scent when I got to the street?"

He corrected her, "I had the instinct you were there. I didn't know for sure. I went across the street to the deli and watched the building entrance from there. Where were you hiding?"

"Do you remember the braided ficus?"

He gave her a blank look. "The what?"

"The potted plant that sat on the floor in the corner of the front hallway and the living room." She fluffed the curls at the back of her neck self-consciously. "I was hiding in the leaves."

A grin broke across his hard features. "Damn, you were right there. Well done. I remember brushing against that tree when I went into the living room. How big are you in your Wyr form?"

She felt a ridiculous burst of pleasure from his praise. "I'm about the length of your forearm. Maybe smaller if I curl my tail up around my body."

"Is that why you have so many potted trees in your living room?" He regarded her with such pleasure that warmth touched her cheeks again.

She nodded and confessed, "Sometimes I like to hang out in the trees while I watch TV."

He burst out laughing. "Of course, why not?" Startled, she felt even more self-conscious. He told her, "Sometimes my wolf likes to hang out and chew on a bone. There are these really tasty beef-basted ones you can get at Wyr Foods."

She smiled. Wyr Foods was a specialty spin-off of the Whole Foods grocery chain. She shopped there, too. She looked at the items she had pulled out of the fridge. A carton of eggs, a package of bacon, veggies, cheese. All right. It looked like she was making an omelet. Wait, she had a couple packages of hash browns in the freezer. She guessed he could eat the full dozen eggs, plenty of bacon, both packages of hash browns, and have room to enjoy toast as well.

She pulled out an omelet pan, a skillet for the bacon, and a sauté pan with deeper sides for the hash browns. Then she rinsed vegetables for the omelet and began to chop them—onion, green bell pepper, mushrooms, and tomatoes.

Gideon watched her work. She looked calmer and more peaceful already as she moved with confidence around her kitchen. Come to think of it, he felt calmer and more peaceful just watching her. She was a beautiful woman in a wholly understated way. It showed in the graceful movements of her slim hands and the delicate bones of her wrists, in the quiet dignity in her intelligent face and that wholly incongruous, wild thing going on with her rich dark hair.

He loved that hair. He had an insane desire, akin to the wolf's running fits—he wanted to pull every one of those corkscrew curls out and watch them spring back into place, to bury his face in it and tickle her until her sadness and dignity broke apart and she laughed herself breathless.

His cock had stiffened again. *Donkey's round hairy ass.* He took a deep breath and flipped one of the chairs around so he could sit in it backward. It had the benefit of hiding the bulge in his jeans. He crossed his arms across the back of the chair and dangled his bottle of Corona from the fingers of one hand. He took a pull from his drink and drop-kicked his mind back to work.

He said, "Ready to continue?"

Alice didn't look up from her vegetable chopping. She nodded.

"Do you know about what happened in Florida seven years ago?"

Her mouth tightened. "Every rainbow chameleon Wyr knows what happened in Florida. They were our friends and family."

Gideon closed his eyes briefly and kicked himself some more. "Of course they were," he said gently.

She scooped the chopped vegetables from the cutting board into a warmed skillet. They sizzled and the aroma of cooking food filled the kitchen. She said, "Do you think it's the same killer?"

Why prevaricate? He said, "Yeah, I do. Since the Jacksonville killer was never caught, a lot of the details from those murders were never released but whoever killed Haley used the same methodology."

She sent him a wide-eyed glance. "Methodology?"

"The killer was very methodical. He masked his scent with a chemical agent that hunters use, and while we don't have a crime scene report yet on Haley, I'm betting he didn't leave any fingerprints behind. The Jacksonville killer didn't either. Each victim died by a stab wound to the heart. It's very neatly done, then their abdominal cavities are excavated. The organs are always placed outside their bodies in the same pattern."

Her hand, still holding the spatula, dropped to her side as her face worked. He moved across the room fast to hold her from behind in a firm grip. She whispered, "H-Haley was dead before he did that to her?"

"Yes," he said in a strong voice. "The killer has some other agenda besides torture. I promise you, Alice. She didn't suffer."

She breathed hard, fighting for control. She said, "Thank you for that. I'm all right."

He released her and stepped back. Not too far, just a couple of steps. Then he stood out of her line of sight, watching her jerky movements as she cooked with his hands fisted at his sides. There was only so much he could do to help, and it was making him a little bat-shit. "Ready for a break?" he asked, hoping she would say yes.

"No." She looked over her shoulder at him. "Please continue."

"You said your principal, Alex Schaffer, was the one who broke the news of Peter Baines' death to you and Haley, and he's also the one who spread the news that David Brunswick had gone missing, correct?" He waited for her nod then continued. "Why Schaffer?"

"After Jacksonville, Alex started a support group for chameleon Wyr. First it was to help process the grief, but over time the group has turned more social. Now we have a potluck on the first Sunday of every month, and some of us get together for brunch on the third Sunday. Sometimes some of us arrange to go hiking, or to go out to dinner or see a movie."

"True Colors," Gideon said.

She looked at him in surprise. "You know the group? We keep its existence pretty quiet. There's a website where everybody can log in and post news, email each other, or invite people on an outing, but it's privately maintained. It doesn't even come up on Google searches."

He told her, "The FBI keeps a file on chameleon Wyr social activities, which includes information on the website. I had a look at it earlier today, but I haven't had time to read through everything. I didn't know Schaffer was the founder of the group."

"Yes, and as far as I know, every chameleon Wyr in New York is a member."

"Twenty-three," Gideon murmured.

"I beg your pardon?" Alice handed him plates, cutlery and napkins.

He set the table. "The website has a list of all your names. The group has twenty-three members." Well, technically the total was now twenty, but he wasn't going to be pedantic about that when it might cause her more pain. "What brought you to Haley's earlier?"

"We had planned to spend the evening together. I was going to try to coax her into coming to stay at my place for a while." He came back toward her, and she handed him the salt and pepper shakers, a bottle of ketchup, and a freshly opened bottle of Corona.

"Did anybody else know you two had planned to get together this evening?" He carried the beer and the condiments to the table.

"No." She frowned up at him. "Does that matter?"

"Maybe, maybe not. Let's keep that private for now, okay?" Could withholding the information be useful? He tucked the thought away for further consideration.

"All right." She slid the last of the bacon out of the skillet, clearly deep in thought. "How did you know to show up at Haley's?"

He smiled at her. "Why don't I tell you that later? You may not need a break, but I do. Just until we've had a chance to eat."

She sighed. "Okay."

He'd lied, but she didn't appear to notice. He could have talked details about the case and autopsy results throughout the meal and never turned a hair, but he wanted her to relax enough to eat a bite or two. A fresh shock wasn't going to help her do that.

Because the police had already found David Brunswick's body in the basement garage of his brownstone, and the killer was in fact exceedingly methodical.

Even though all of the Jacksonville murders were found at the same time, one of the details suppressed by the authorities was that the group had been held prisoner for a while at their enclave. At first the scene indicated a mass murder, but it soon became apparent that serial tendencies were involved, as the killer had ritually dissected one person each day until all seven were dead. The autopsy results confirmed the succession of murders. The report listed the victims by the date of their deaths, and the names were in alphabetical order.

That afternoon, Gideon had looked at the list of group members on the True Colors website. Peter Baines, David Brunswick. The third on the list was Haley Cannes. He had called the school but Haley had already left work.

He thought he might have dreams about moving as fast and as hard as he could to her Brooklyn address only to arrive too late. If only he had pieced it together a few hours earlier, Alice's friend would still be alive. Maybe Haley would even be sitting down to supper with them.

He helped Alice carry the food to the table. She had cooked a dozen eggs with the sautéed vegetables. The intended omelet became a scramble upon which she had heaped scoops of sour cream and cheese. The hash browns were a delectable brown, and the bacon was so aromatic and crispy, his stomach emitted a loud rumble.

He gave her a sheepish grin and Alice laughed. Then she said suddenly, "Oh, I forgot to make toast!"

He snagged her by putting an arm around her shoulders and redirecting her back to the table. "Please sit and relax. This is more than perfect."

She frowned at him over the delicate wire-rims perched on her slender nose. "As long as you're sure."

He clenched down on an almost uncontrollable urge to kiss her. It wasn't time.

Not yet, at any rate.

He said, "I'm sure."

He held Alice's chair for her. She smiled at him as he sat. "Don't be shy," she said. "Eat up. As you can see, I cooked portions relative to your size."

So she had. He inhaled deeply as he looked at the fragrant meal. Gods above, he didn't even have to taste any of it to know she was a superb cook. He told her, "This is more heaven than I can remember seeing in one place for quite some time. Please serve yourself something before I get started."

Her gorgeous cocoa-and-cream skin turned pink with pleasure. "I'm not very hungry but, well, okay."

She took a little of the scrambled eggs, a slice of bacon, and a spoonful of the hash browns. It was not nearly enough to his critical gaze, but on a night that was so hard for her, it probably would have to do.

She might lose her appetite for even that small amount if she were to realize hers was the fourth name on that website list.

Not that anything was going to happen to her. Not on Gideon's watch. He would die before he let that happen.

Chapter Four

The Depths

---

*T*rue *north.*

What the hell did it mean?

Gideon could wish for a little time to contemplate it. For now, though, he shoveled half the contents of each skillet on to his plate, helped himself to a generous squirt of ketchup on the hash browns and set to with enthusiasm.

Those first quick bites were indescribably delicious. Salty meat, rich melted cheese and sour cream on eggs and veggies, and crunchy filling potatoes, all with a beautiful, gentle woman in a warm kitchen on a cold winter's night. Suddenly Gideon felt happier than he ever thought possible, happier than was even comfortable. The emotion shuddered through him with such fierce intensity his fingers shook as he gripped his knife and fork. He clenched his hands, willing the unsteadiness to stop.

Gideon had been one of Cuelebre's deadliest dogs of war, the alpha captain that led the wolves, the mastiffs and the mongrels. His brigade had been the most gifted and volatile, the troops on the extreme edge. They had hurtled first into any conflict, not baying, but racing to the battle in an eager, murderous silence. They were the advance scouts, the rangers sent in to places too dangerous for the regular troops, the sentries that patrolled the shadowed corners and slipped past enemy lines to take down their opponents from behind.

Gideon had risen in the ranks when he still had the thoughtless athleticism of youth and a strong body that could go on forever just because he asked it to. Now that boundless, youthful energy had turned to disciplined maturity, and his blond hair had faded like an aging golden retriever's pelt. He exercised and trained hard to maintain his muscled physique, stamina and quick reflexes. Each battle he fought and won, he did so knowing that his youth might have gone but he was still at peak condition, and it was not yet time for the alpha to lose his place at the head of the pack.

He was not one of the strange, immortal Wyr who had come into existence in the dawn of the world. Wolf Wyr had a life span of around two hundred years. If something didn't bring him down first he expected to see another good eighty, eight-five years. With discipline and constant training, he could have spent another fifty years in active combat duty before age would have forced him to consider other options.

Here in the gentle sanctuary of Alice's kitchen decorated with pretty sunflowers and sage green cabinets, with her sensitive, bright hazel gaze resting on him thoughtfully, and the kindest, most generous and delicious meal anybody had ever cooked for him spread out before him, he could finally admit the truth to himself about why he had quit—he had grown tired.

The tips of her slender fingers touched the back of one of his hands. "Are you all right?"

Riehl ducked his head. "Yeah," he said, his voice gruff. "Thank you for supper."

"You're welcome." The tip of her tongue touched her lower lip. She looked as if she wanted to say something else, but she lowered her head instead.

They ate supper in a silence that was surprisingly comfortable. When Alice finished the food on her plate, Gideon took the serving spoon and offered her another helping of the scrambled egg dish. She raised her eyebrows but nodded with a smile. He watched with deep pleasure as she ate it.

His cell rang with Bayne's ringtone, the Bee Gee's "Stayin' Alive". He ducked his head further to shovel the last of the hash browns into his mouth even as he dug into his pocket for his phone. "Sorry," he muttered. "It's my boss. I've got to get this."

The shadows came back into her face. He hated to see that. She said, "Of course you do."

Gideon strode into the living room and clicked on the phone. "Yeah."

"Heard you found your witness," said Bayne.

"Yeah, I'm still with her," Gideon said. He started to pace. "We're at her place. What's up?"

"We're wrapping up at Haley Cannes' apartment." The gryphon said to someone else, "Pack it up. I want someone to comb through every file on the hard drive, and check out every contact on her email list." Then his voice came back stronger, "You find out anything from Alice Clark?"

Hell yeah, a whole slew of new things, but most of them weren't any of the sentinel's business. Gideon turned to pace another lap. Alice was cleaning up the kitchen. She had carried the dishes to the sink. Even though she had a dishwasher, she was running a sink full of soapy water. It looked like she felt the need to do something as well.

Gideon said, "We're still talking."

"Call or text if you find out something new. In the meantime, we've got a lock on the whereabouts of all the chameleon Wyr who live in NYC. Now that schools have let out for winter break, some are traveling for the holidays. A family of four has left for Arizona, a single parent, her boyfriend and her kid have gone to L.A., and a couple are headed for Miami. We're checking with the airports to confirm their flights left before the storm shut things down, but assuming they did, that leaves us eleven chameleons still in the city."

"Right." He looked at Alice again. She had finished the dishes and was wiping off the table. She had just started winter break? On the one hand, he liked that she had personal time right now. She needed it. On the other, he didn't like the thought of her possible isolation. He growled, "Eleven is more than enough if he's looking to do a repeat of seven years ago."

"He'd only need four more, wouldn't he?" Bayne said. "Something bothers me about all this. If this is the

Jacksonville guy, last time he took advantage of a situation that was very comfortable for him. All of his victims lived together in one place, and they tended to isolate so nobody knew something might be wrong when the group disappeared for a week. They were only found after acquaintances missed them at the Masque they had scheduled to attend. That's not the case with these murders."

Gideon rubbed the back of his neck. "He plots things out carefully ahead of time," he said. "He's got a plan and he thinks it's going to work."

"Yeah," Bayne growled. "That bothers me a hell of a lot."

That also bothered Gideon. He asked, "What about protection?" The NYPD wouldn't have the funding to provide police protection for eleven people, but the Wyr Division of Violent Crime was supported by a separate funding stream that came from the demesne's coffers. As the sentinel heading the WDVC, Bayne could authorize such an expenditure of manpower and money if he deemed it appropriate.

"I'll be setting up a task force when I get back to the office," said Bayne. "Protection's at the top of the agenda. It should be in place for everyone by morning. I want you to head it up."

Gideon stopped pacing at the instant surge of denial. He looked at Alice again, and said to Bayne, "No can do. You'll have to find someone else."

Bayne said, "I assume you have a compelling reason for turning down this urgent assignment, and you are willing to share that reason with your new boss."

"I do indeed," said Gideon. "But it's difficult to go into detail right now. I'll have to get back to you."

"Is that some kind of secret code for she can hear everything you say?"

"Yeah, something like that. In the meantime, I need to get back to questioning Alice."

"Has she figured out she's next on the list?"

"I don't know," Gideon said. "Maybe. But it's all right, since I will be spending the night."

Alice lifted her head and turned to look at him, her eyes wide and startled.

"I was going to tell you to hang with her until I got a guard detail sent over," Bayne grunted. "At least that's one thing to cross off my list tonight."

"You can take it one step further," Gideon told him. "I'll stay the point person on this assignment."

There was a long pause on the other end. "Are there implications in that?" Bayne asked. "I don't like implications. I can't figure them out on my own very often."

Gideon smiled at Alice reassuringly. He said to Bayne. "Talk to you soon."

"You'd better, son. You've got a lot to tell me," said Bayne, who then hung up.

Alice's pulse roared in her ears as she watched Gideon pocket his cell phone. She looked down and realized she was twisting the dish towel in her hands. She fought to breathe evenly as she hung the towel on the stove handle. Clothing whispered as Gideon moved into the kitchen doorway. There had to be something sane and sensible she could say, if only she could think of it. Her rabbiting mind hopped through a series of statements and discarded each one in rapid-fire succession.

That's pretty presumptuous of you there, Detective. Did I say I'd let you spend the night?

Of course you've got to stay the night. It's too dangerous out for anyone to try to drive.

How about that storm, eh?

We haven't even kissed yet. (NOOO. Don't say that.)

She croaked, "Do you want coffee?"

"Alice," said Gideon.

Her head jerked up.

Watching her, Gideon felt such a powerful surge of tenderness at the disturbed confusion on her face, he couldn't even smile, and for once the inappropriate lust stayed subjugated to his will. He wanted to take her in his arms again, just to hold her and tell her that everything would be all right.

He told her in a gentle voice, "I'm sorry I didn't get a chance to talk things over with you first, but my boss and I would like for me to crash on your couch tonight."

Her unsteady fingers smoothed the towel. "You think that's best?"

"We do," he said. "There are too many indications that the killer feels the compulsion to follow certain patterns of order."

"What do you mean?" Her fingers stilled. "Do you think he has obsessive-compulsive tendencies?"

"He might. He's undeniably bright and capable of a great deal of organization, so he also might be able to hide his true nature under an appearance of normality. The ability of concealment that some psychopaths have is what psychiatrist Hervey Cleckley referred to when he first coined the term 'mask of sanity' in 1941." Gideon took a deep breath and forced himself to continue. "A lot of details from Jacksonville have never been released because the killer hasn't yet been caught. He held the group prisoner and executed one a day. They were killed in alphabetical order."

He noted the moment that realization struck. She sucked in a harsh, shaking breath and looked up again. Then he couldn't hold back any further. He strode over to take hold of her slender shoulders in a firm, reassuring grip.

"Which is *not* going to happen this time," he said strongly into her whitened face. "It's also quite apparent that the number seven has a great deal of significance for him."

"It's significant to all the Elder Races," Alice murmured. "Seven demesnes in the U.S., seven Primal Powers or gods."

"The previous murders occurred in the days leading up to the Festival of the Masque," Gideon continued. "So we think that the seven gods have some particular meaning for him. He murdered seven people in seven days. Now, seven years later, the murders have started again. He excavates seven organs from his victims—the liver, gall bladder, pancreas, the two kidneys, the spleen, and he goes up under the rib cage to remove the heart. And he places the organs in a distinct pattern, although we haven't figured out what the significance of that is yet."

His hands on her shoulders were massive and warm. She gripped his forearms, and the feeling of his warm skin over solid muscle steadied her again. Her mind arrowed back to that terrible stillness in Haley's apartment, but when she recalled the gaping dark red hole in Haley's midsection she froze and couldn't force herself to go any further.

She said through gritted teeth, "I can't see it. I don't remember. Does he always use the same pattern?"

He hesitated and his striking pale eyes searched her face. He said heavily, "Yeah. The heart is in the center, with the other organs set around it."

She frowned up at him, her mouth held so tight her lips were bloodless. "How are they positioned?"

She could see him warring with the impulse to protect her from the details. Finally he said, "He puts the liver at twelve o'clock, spleen at six, and the gall bladder and pancreas at three and nine o'clock respectively."

"The four directions," she said.

"Excuse me?" he asked, taken aback. Her gaze was still trained on him but he didn't think she saw him.

"Seven gods. Seven. Four. Two." She asked, "Where does he place the two kidneys?"

His expression grew intent. "On either side of the liver, at the top of the circle."

"I know that pattern," Alice said. "I use it all the time."

He stared at her. His grip on her shoulders tightened. Then he let her go and stepped back. "Show me."

She rushed from the kitchen. Gideon strode after her, watching her mutter to herself. She moved down the short hall and flipped on a light to the front bedroom. She had turned it into a home office, with a computer desk and chair against one wall, and a futon set in a couch position against another wall. Like Haley, Alice had pulled out boxes of Masque decorations. They were set in the middle of the floor. She dropped to her knees in front of one box and dug through it.

"It's a silly hobby of mine," she said over her shoulder. "I don't really know a lot about it. I just dabble, not like some people. Every year we hold a Winter Solstice Masque as a fundraiser for the school. I give Tarot readings—I use the Primal Tarot, of course, not any of the European decks. Those came later, around the fifteenth century, I think. The Primal Tarot is much, much older. I only know half a dozen of the most used card spreads."

He rubbed the back of his neck as he listened to her rapid speech. "You're talking about fortune telling?"

She emerged from the cardboard box with a smaller hand-painted wooden box clutched in one hand. Her cheeks flushed. "Actually, historically it was used for divination and considered a serious religious matter. If it was done in a prayerful manner, it was supposed to be a way for the gods to speak to us," she said. "It was only in the nineteenth century that it became more like the fortune telling one might find at a carnival. I don't have any Power for real divination nor do I practice it as a religion. I just do a carnival-like show. I can make twenty-five bucks for a fifteen-minute reading. It's very popular at school. Usually I end up with several hundred dollars at the end of the night."

"Okay," he said. He squatted in front of her. "Why don't you show me what you're talking about?"

She sat cross-legged on the carpet, opened the box and pulled out an old deck of cards. Gideon settled on the floor opposite her. He picked up the box that she had put to one side. It was made of cedar and a faint Power thrummed gently in his hands, old Power that had saturated the aged wood. He considered the painting on the top. It was white and royal blue and gold, with outlines of black and a small highlight of crimson. The colors must have been brilliant once, but they had faded over time. The painting was of a stylized face. One side was male and the other side female.

"This is Taliesin, right?" he asked. He wasn't very religious, but he knew at least that much. To the Elder Races, the seven Primal Powers were the linchpins of the universe. Each Power had a persona, or a mask of personality. Both male and female, Taliesin was the first among the gods of the Elder Races, the Supreme Power to which all others bowed.

"Yes," Alice said. "Isn't it amazing? The whole deck is hand-painted. I found it in an antique store about twelve years ago." She touched the corner of the box as he held it. "I fell in love and ended up paying far too much for it. I ate a lot of macaroni and cheese that year."

He set the box aside with care and turned his attention to Alice.

"The Primal Tarot has forty-nine cards in the deck," she said. "The Major Arcana in this Tarot are the seven gods in their prime aspects—or how most people know of them." She set the first card on floor between them and named it. "Taliesin, the god of the Dance, is first among the Primal Powers because everything dances, the planets and all the stars, other gods, ourselves. Dance is change, and the universe is constantly in motion. Then there's Azrael, the god of Death; Inanna, the goddess of Love; Nadir, the goddess of the depths or the Oracle— legend has it that Nadir is the one who gave the Primal Tarot to the Elder Races."

"When was that supposed to have happened?" he asked.

"Around the third century, or at least that's the age of the earliest known Primal Tarot. Then there is Will, the god of the Gift; Camael, the goddess of the Hearth; and Hyperion, the god of Law."

He studied each card as she laid them out, the famous green eyes of Death, the seven royal lions that pulled Inanna's chariot, the dark sense of vastness captured in the stars in Nadir's gaze. The cards were arresting but not quite beautiful. They were too uncomfortable for that.

He murmured, "Someone with real Power used these once."

"I think it's the person who created them," Alice said. "The rest of the cards are the Minor Arcana. The gods have their major aspects, and then they have all their minor aspects. Take Azrael. Death is his major aspect, but in the Tarot deck, he has six other minor aspects. He's also the god of regeneration and green growing things, and he's known as the Hunter, and he's also the Gateway or passage. See?"

"Yes," Gideon said. He was growing fascinated despite himself.

"Inanna's easy, her minor aspects are Love in its manifestations—romantic, platonic, etc.—and also love's opposite, which is apathy. Taliesin's major aspect is the dance, or change, but there's also stasis, or the pauses between measures in the dance. Some of Will's other aspects are the wanderer or sacred stranger, and sacrifice, and also greed." As she talked, she laid out the Minor Arcana in lateral rows underneath the Major cards, six under each, until all forty-nine were placed on the floor. "Camael has both the sacred fool and old wisdom, and Hyperion may be law, but he's also the trickster."

"So where do the four and the two come in?" he asked.

"They come in the spreads." She gathered the cards up and shuffled them swiftly. "There are three classical card spreads used in Primal Tarot readings, but really it's just one original spread with more detail added in the other two. All the other card spreads were created or invented some time after the original three. The person who gets the reading is supposed to be the one to shuffle the cards and lay them out. The first card is called the Primus, or the primary force or influence in one's life at the time of the reading. Sometimes it's called the keystone card of the spread. The interpretation of all the other cards is always based on this one."

She pulled out a card and laid it on the floor. They gazed down at Azrael's emerald green painted eyes.

Lord Death.

"Well, that's more apropos today than I would have liked," she muttered. "There are three layers to a spread—the Primus, Secondus and Tertius—and it matters if a card is right-side up, or reversed. The top part is what you're working toward, either a goal or some unforeseen event. The bottom is where you're coming from. The right side has negative influences, and the left is positive. The last two cards at the top actually have to do with the future." She set down the last card and looked at Gideon. "Is that the pattern you were talking about?"

He stared down at the cards. "Hell yeah," he said. "That's it. He's attempting divination. That's why he does it in the days leading up to the Masque. The bastard's trying to talk with the gods."

Chapter Five

The Dance

Gideon shocked her when he leaned forward and planted a swift kiss on her forehead. "You're miraculous," he said. He smiled, nose-to-nose with her, and she smiled back. "Do you know how many fancy PhDs and profilers have studied the Jacksonville case and never got that? I've got to call Bayne."

He strode out of the room. Full of warmth from his praise, Alice looked down at the full card spread for the first time. Her smile slipped away and she went numb.

All seven of the Death cards were laid out. It was a pure spread.

She had never seen a pure spread before, just as she had never seen a royal flush in poker. Today seemed to be a day of rare firsts. Normally she would have contemplated the spread and let her mind roam free to let the whisper of Power in the cards tell her what they would. While she had told Gideon the truth and she didn't have much Power, the cards sometimes had a mind of their own.

But she couldn't handle the implications of this kind of reading tonight. Her mind felt bruised and dull, incapable of hearing the still, small voice in the cards. If they had anything to say to her, it was going to have to wait. She scooped up the deck, tucked it away in the silk-lined box, and pushed to her feet with the slow, awkward movements of the emotionally and physically exhausted.

Gideon had moved to the kitchen. She could hear him pacing and talking. He had frightened her so much just hours earlier. How had his huge, energetic presence become such a comfort so quickly? She knew if he wasn't already planning to spend the night, she would ask him to stay.

She went to the living room and lay down on the couch. She curled on her side to watch the gas flames and listen to the sound of his deep, gravelly voice.

Death and death and death. Death in the past, Peter and David. Death in the present, Haley. Death as the overriding force in her life, and death in her future. She had a killer on her side, and the Hunter as her challenge. She closed her eyes. She wanted so very much to turn her mind off.

She had the sense of something massive looming over her. She opened her eyes. Gideon bent over her. His hard face was softened into an expression of such kindness that her eyes watered. He stroked a curl at her temple. "What can I do for you?"

"Nothing, thanks. I'm just tired," she told him. She pushed to a sitting position.

"And sad. I would like to see you happy, someday soon." He cupped her cheek with long calloused fingers. "It's almost one o'clock, and we're done. Do you think you could sleep?"

She nodded. "I'll get you some things, some bedding—"

"Don't worry about me," he said. The tough line of his sexy mouth pulled into a smile. "I have a toiletry kit in the Jeep that I'm going to get and then, if you don't mind, I thought I might let my wolf out. He has a hankering to snooze by your fire if you'll let him."

She had no idea where her barriers had gone. They had simply vanished like morning mist. She put a hand over his and let her feelings show in her gaze. "I'd love to meet your wolf. I'm so sorry that we met the way we did, but I'm very glad we did."

"That's good to hear, sweetheart," he said. He bent forward that little bit further and put his mouth over hers. It was a warm, tender, chaste kiss, and so utterly perfect for who and where she was at that moment.

She gave herself another gift: she leaned forward and kissed him back, touching his lean cheek with light, tentative fingers, and let herself trust in him.

He pulled back and growled softly, "Okay, Alice, fair warning. That's as good as I'm ever going to get. You should know, most of the time I'm actually a bit of a shit."

She shocked herself by bursting out laughing.

He gave her a lopsided grin. "Go get ready for bed," he told her. "I'm going to get my kit. I'll be right back."

She watched him walk to the door. When he unlocked it and made as if to walk out just in his t-shirt, she asked, "Aren't you going to put on your coat?" The temperature outside had to be subzero by now.

The glance he shot at her was icy pale but burning hot. "I could use a blast of cold air right now."

Her breath shuddered in her throat.

Me, she thought. He means because of me.

He pulled open the door. As he went out a sword-like thrust of wind screamed into the apartment. She shot off the couch and retreated to the relative warmth and privacy of her bathroom.

After inspecting her hollow-eyed face in the bathroom mirror, she brushed her teeth and took a quick five-minute shower to wash away the grime of the city. Her lemon-yellow, thigh-length nightgown and dark blue robe hung from a hook on the bathroom door. She slipped them on and walked out of the bathroom.

Fifteen feet away in the living room, a white-blond wolf lay facing the bathroom door with his head on his paws.

She lost her breath.

He was enormous, easily twice the size of a mundane wolf, heavily muscled across the chest and rib cage with long, strong, powerful-looking legs. His eyes were the same icy pale blue as they were when he was in his human form. As she stared at the wolf, his tail waved gently. Despite his ferocious appearance and intimidating size, somehow he managed to seem diffident.

Gideon said in her head, *I thought it might be a good idea for you to meet the wolf this way before you went to bed. I don't want to scare you if you get up in the middle of the night. I don't have to stay this way if it's not all right.*

All right? He was the most beautiful thing she had ever seen, and the most dangerous. She fell to her knees and held out a hand. "You're gorgeous," she told the wolf. "You couldn't be more perfect."

The wolf's eyes brightened. He stood—good *night*, he kept going up and up—and padded over slowly. She realized he was giving her time to change her mind.

She didn't change her mind. As soon as he came close enough to touch, she ran a light hand over his thick pelt. It felt soft and luxuriant, even springy under her palm. He side-stepped closer, nosed at her hand and licked her fingers with such open affection, she laughed again in surprised delight.

She gave herself another gift, threw caution out the window and hugged him. She felt the careful shift in his body as he leaned against her just a little, not too much, and he put his head on her shoulder. She rubbed her face in his fur. He threw off heat like a radiator. His big, warm presence filled places inside of her she hadn't known were empty.

"Thank you for staying," she whispered.

I wouldn't want to be anywhere else, he said quietly. He nuzzled her. *Go to bed now. You're safe.*

Something coiled tight inside of her unwound. She sagged against his powerful, sturdy body and nodded. Then she climbed to her feet, passed her hand over the wolf's head in one last caress, and went into her shadowed room to climb into bed.

Exhaustion swirled around her as her head hit the pillow. She heard quiet sounds as Gideon moved through the apartment, and she knew he was checking the windows and doors.

She thought the wolf might have padded into her room to touch the index finger of her out-flung hand with his cold nose, but she might have been dreaming at that point. In her dream, the wolf rested his head on the edge of the bed and gazed at her with a devotion she would have believed impossible before that day. Then someone turned out all the lights in her head, and she slept.

Waking wasn't a good experience. It came hard and fast. She surfaced out of a nightmare with the chill of clammy skin and the wicked whiplash of wind snapping just outside her bedroom window.

She had kicked off all her covers and curled into a tight ball. She forced her muscles to unclench. She rolled to look over the edge of the bed at the floor. No wolf. Of course he wasn't there. He would be in front of the fire, where he said he would be.

The blurry letters on her bedside clock read 3:23 AM. The room felt empty and cold, the shelter from the storm all too insubstantial. Her nightmare had been full of dark, wet knives, and she missed him. She just missed him.

She didn't give herself time to fight the impulse. She slipped her glasses on her nose, grabbed the top blanket as she climbed out of bed and walked into the living room.

There she found everything in the world. Warmth and light from the fire flickered over the massive body of the wolf that lay on the floor stretched out on his side. His clothes were folded in a neat pile nearby, his holstered gun resting on top. His half-closed eyes shifted but he held still as she lay down on the floor behind him. She set her glasses on the nearby coffee table, dragged the blanket around her and curled shivering against the wolf's broad, warm back.

Gideon's mental voice rumbled quietly in her head. *Bad dream?*

"Yeah," she whispered. She rubbed her face in his fur.

The powerful muscles in his back tensed. *Is it all right if I change?*

She nodded. "I can't remember the last nightmare I had," she said. "I'm not usually a needy person—"

Hush, sweetheart.

The wolf rolled on to his stomach. He shimmered into the change. Whatever else she had meant to say flew out of her head as Gideon's massive, nude human body lay stretched out before her. Gold light played over the broad muscles of his long back and spilled into the graceful hollow of his lower spine, his buttocks and strong, heavy thighs. He was lean everywhere, the taut covering of his tanned skin rippling over the flex of thick muscle and fluid shift of bone as he came up on his elbows to look at her.

The expression on his hard, lean face was serious, concerned. Her throat closed on a lump as he rolled over and gathered her against his chest. "I'm glad you're not a needy person," he murmured. His voice rumbled against her cheek. "But I want you to need me. Don't apologize or prevaricate. Just need me."

"It's so scary," she breathed. "When I ate lunch yesterday, I didn't know you existed."

He cradled her head in one hand and leaned over her. His pale gaze glittered like aquamarines. "Yesterday is gone. Who we are to each other today and who we will be tomorrow—those are the things that matter."

She read the lines and marks on his harsh face with the tips of her fingers, and stroked down the long, strong column of his throat. A heavy, hard length grew against her thigh, and it felt strange and new, but at the same time so familiar and necessary.

She looked at him in naked bewilderment. "I don't understand how any of this happened," she said, through trembling lips. "We haven't even kissed yet. I mean, we have, but not really."

A fine tremor ran through the big hand that cradled her head and his face flushed with raw, sensual hunger. He closed his eyes and growled, "Your last few days have been so hellish. I'm trying to be so goddamn careful and give you what you need—"

She touched his mouth in wonder. She thought, I dreamed that a wolf came to my bed and watched over me while I slept. There was an epic story in those silent eyes, of mountains that had been crossed and a world that had been fought, and countless years that had been spent in service and in solitude. And there was a promise in that wolf's eyes, a promise from an old warrior soul that knew what it meant to dig down deep and hold true to what he claimed no matter what.

She heard herself ask, "Did you come into my bedroom earlier?"

I dreamed a dream of passion, devotion and loyalty, and a promise that meant everything—

The shaking in his hands increased. He whispered against her fingers, "Just to make sure you were okay. Whatever you want, whatever you need. Tell me and I'll give it to you."

Everything.

And for one shining moment, her world became simple and clean and good again.

"I need you," she said.

She felt the breath leave his body. His eyes opened, and the expression in them blazed. How she could have ever thought those pale blue eyes were icy, she would never know. They burned with a pure, steady flame.

Her hands slipped away from his face as he brought his mouth down on hers, and the warm impact of his lips caused her eyes to flutter shut. She was cradled from behind and caressed from above, and all the while she knew that the heavy, hard weight of him hovered over her, balanced for the moment but ready to fall. Her hands landed on the heavy, wide arc of his collarbones and slipped down the expanse of his pectorals, while her mouth formed a soft 'o' of surprise for how good it was, how incredibly good—

—and he took that as his invitation to slip inside. He curled his tongue between her lips with a sensual gentleness that spoke of infinite care and deep emotion.

She learned something from his kiss and took it to heart. This man felt things he never spoke of verbally. Instead he said them with his body and his eyes, his mouth and his hands, and in that moment as she kissed him back, she made a silent promise to him to learn the language he spoke so that she heard everything he had to say to her.

Then his language changed and became harder, more demanding. He spoke of need too, as he drove his hardened tongue into her mouth and shoved a heavy thigh between her legs. His massive body became a silent shout of urgency. He rocked his hips against hers, massaging the hot length of his cock against the arc of her pelvis, and the shudder of his breath blasted against her cheek as he cupped one of her breasts and fingered her erect, aching nipple through the thin nightgown.

She caught fire. It ran shining like liquid mercury through her veins. She arched into his touch and groaned as she gripped the back of his head. Her hands slipped against the short corn silk of his pale hair.

"Tell me to stop, sweetheart," he muttered against her cheek. "Just say the word if we're going too fast."

His body said something else though, as he ground harder against her.

It said, *please, please.*

She stroked the wide arc of his back as she whispered in his ear, "You are my mate. I could never say no to you."

His head reared back. He stared at her in astonishment.

For one terrible moment, dread darkened her vision and her heart gave a sickened lurch. She thought, I cannot be so wrong. I cannot live with it if I am so deluded.

The joy that came over his face was so incandescent, it blinded her. "That's what it means," he said. "True north."

She broke into a bout of reactive shivering. "What?"

He leaned on one elbow to caress her face. "When I looked at you for the first time, the world changed. It all but knocked me off my feet. I've been thinking it was like true north had shifted, the magnetic pull from the one direction you use in navigation, but it's more like the primary force from your card spread. I've been trying to figure out what it meant. All I knew was that it was you—you had become my true north, my primary force. Just like that, from one moment to the next."

She closed her eyes and swallowed hard as the world came back into focus. "Yes, that's what happened to me too."

He bent down to nuzzle her neck. "It reminds me of a quote from a French philosopher. 'The heart has reasons that reason cannot know.' Do you know it?"

She wound her arms around his neck, and she let her frightened heart find ease and grow full of him. "I do now."

I dreamed a dream of incomparable rarity and loveliness.

Then I woke to find it true.

Chapter Six

Sacrifice

Gideon stared at the woman in his arms. She was so gorgeous it took his breath. He had thought her beauty was understated and intelligent, but right at that moment she was so flagrant with color and voluptuousness he could only gaze at her in passionate awe.

Her cocoa-and-cream skin turned a deep rich gold in the light of the fire, and her vivid eyes shone blue and green. Those fabulous gold-tipped corkscrew curls spilled extravagantly over his hands, and her pale yellow nightgown moved like silk against his overheated skin. Her breasts were full and generous, and the dark areola of her erect nipples pushed against the thin material.

He imagined watching her grow older, a pale sprinkling of frost touching those curls, the laugh lines growing at the corners of her eyes and that delicate, sensitive mouth. The images in his imagination drew him at a fundamental level. She could only become lovelier to him as he grew to know her with the intimacy of the passing years.

He bent his head and caressed the slender arc of her golden neck with his lips. He felt the sigh of pleasure that shuddered through her, the sexy shift of her body molding to fit his, and oh holy gods, he was the one who did that to her, great hulking brute that he was. The wonder of it closed his throat.

He knew too much about how to kill and hardly anything about how to live in peace. Hell, he hardly knew how to stay indoors for any length of time. She was too good for him, too refined. She put cloth napkins on her table, read books of poetry, and taught small children. The quilts she created were works of art that nurtured the soul.

He put bullets in clips to load his guns, and read files on unsolved crimes and treatises on war. He taught recruits how to wait, how to obey orders, and how to kill, and he played chess because it was a battle of wits that kept his mind sharp.

He put his forehead to her breast. His hands fisted in her nightgown.

He needed to come home but he didn't know how. He hadn't even known where home was until he looked in her face for the first time. He needed to be welcomed, but he wasn't sure he deserved it.

She had fled her bedroom and her nightmare with a look of surprised horror. But he knew the nightmare she'd had. That nightmare was an old acquaintance of his. The details might change, along with the faces of the victims, but the story remained the same. It was a tale of a fire so dark it burned the soul black.

He *was* that nightmare for some people.

She stroked his hair. "Gideon?"

Christ, now he was responsible for putting that uncertainty in her voice, right at the time when she should be drenched in the knowledge of how lovely, how desirable he found her. He struggled to tell her something, anything, to let her know it could never be anything wrong with her. It was all about what was wrong with him.

He whispered, "I want to be a good man."

Her hands stilled. Then she brought them under his jaw to coax his head up. She searched his expression, her beautiful gaze troubled. "Why would you think you're not a good man?" she asked in a gentle voice.

"I've spent almost a hundred years in the army," he said, his voice strangled. "I've seen things. I've done things you can't imagine. I don't ever want you to be able to imagine them. You deserve someone so much better than me, someone finer who knows how to live your life."

"How do you know you're not that man?" she asked. She reached up to kiss him, the delicate curve of her lips caressing his. "The heart has its reasons, remember?"

A tremor ran through his body. "You don't know, you don't understand."

"You're right, I don't," she told him.

Alice stroked his face and passed a hand down the broad expanse of his back, trying to soothe him. This was the same distress that shook through him earlier at the dining table. It was hard to watch him suffer, especially when she wasn't sure he realized how much he was hurting. "I can't possibly understand."

"I chose it," he said. "I thrived in the army. I was good at it."

He would have been. She could see it. Strong, responsible, stable, reliable as the earth. He would have been the first in battle and the last to pull out, and the need for all of that would have been so self-evident to him, he never would have seen it as sacrifice. True nobility never recognized itself.

She might have acknowledged him as her mate yesterday, but it was in that moment that she fell in love with him.

She said, "I am a person of faith, Gideon. It got rocked a little yesterday, but it is back on solid ground now. I do not believe that we would be mates without also being right for each other. The fates or the gods, or whomever it was that created the Wyr to be what we are, would not have been so cruel."

He muttered, "I don't have your faith. Not after all the atrocities and ugliness I've seen. Wickedness and inequities exist; nightmares are real. And the gods allow all of it." He met her gaze. "But I do know one thing—you're the purest gift I've ever been given, and I'll do anything to keep you safe and be worthy of you." He closed his eyes and turned his face into her palm.

She bit her lip. She could almost see the barrier that surrounded him. He wanted and needed to be with her, but somehow he was still closed off, and she knew she had not quite gotten through to him, not all the way, not yet.

Maybe it would just take time to let the reality of what had happened to them sink in. But maybe...

"You've got to remember, we met when I was having a really off day," she told him. "Because most of the time I'm actually a bit of a shit, too."

His startled gaze snapped up to hers, twin aquamarines frozen in the firelight. She flicked a finger at his nose and rolled her hips at him.

The corners of his sexy mouth began to curl up. He came on top of her more fully, and she parted her legs, knees bent to cradle him with her whole body. It was so good to feel him grip her by one thigh and anchor her down that she moistened for him in a liquid gush. The heavy length of his cock lay against her entrance. He pressed at the place where she was so sensitive she could feel his erection pulse, and she knew in that moment the invisible barrier was gone and he was right there with her, body and soul.

"Care to expound on that statement?" he murmured.

They had so much to learn about each other. The barrier would probably come back. It might take a long time for it to go completely. But for now, she opened her mouth to lick at his lips. "Nah," she said, as she gave him a small grin. "I think you'll see for yourself soon enough."

The crow's feet lines at the corners of his eyes deepened. He bent his head and ran his lips lightly along the skin of her neck, as he whispered, "I can hardly wait."

The warm, moist exhalation of his breath on her sensitized skin was a caress all its own. It had the same effect as touching a match to kindling. Her body flashed hot as if a sheet of flame had doused her, and the hunger she felt for him was so ravening she shook from it. Oh gods, it was stronger than anything she had ever felt before. This feeling was so huge it threatened to swallow her whole.

She'd had lovers. Only a few, but they were enough that she thought she knew what she was about. She tried to brace herself, to hold on to some kind of rational thought or expectation. The first time with a new lover was never all that great. She'd always had to urge them to slow down. They needed time to get to know each other's likes and dislikes before their lovemaking would get really good, and it wouldn't matter in the slightest if he—if he wasn't all that sensually gifted because he was so very fine, just so damn perfect in every other—

He took her nightgown by the neckline and tore it off her. Then he fell on her like a starving man on a feast. His entire tremendous body was ridged with all the heavy muscles held taut, and the look on his face was so desperate and raw that tears sprang to her eyes. His head arrowed down to her breasts, and he licked and suckled at her nipples until they jutted wet and distended, unbearably sensitive nubs of flesh. He moved from one to the other, as he stroked a big hand along the inside of her thighs and teased the private opening of her cleft with shaking fingers. She felt herself moisten further for him until his hand was soaked with her pleasure.

She touched him everywhere she could reach, with her mouth and her hands, arching up to rub her torso along the muscled length of his. He was breathing hard and whining low at the back of his throat, a barely discernible sound that nevertheless caught at her and pulled her outside of herself. When she groped between them to grip the heavy, hard shaft of his penis, he froze with a groan.

She looked into his pale, burning gaze as she fingered his erection, learning him by touch. His skin was flushed dark, the bones of his face clenched. Her hands were shaking, too. He felt huge to her, the length of his cock thick, ridged with veins and capped with a broad head with velvet soft skin. They both looked down the space between their bodies. Her slender legs were splayed wide for him, her delicate flesh plump, moist and inviting.

The emptiness at that juncture became a spike of need. She tugged on him gently, letting her hand stroke along the length of him. "Come inside," she whispered. "We can go slow some other time."

He shook his head, his breath coming in short hard pants, even as his hips pumped a slow grind that thrust his cock into her fist. "Not too fast. Not—God!"

The agonized pleasure that crossed his face as she massaged him was the most exquisite thing she'd ever seen. Her need spiked higher, hotter. She was so empty she hurt. She sucked air and struggled to articulate. "Gideon, please."

He met her gaze quickly. "Does it ache, sweetheart?"

His desperation had not gone. He held it in check, and the tenderness and heat in his eyes made the easy swell of her tears spill over. She nodded jerkily.

He bent and nuzzled at her breast, and whispered, "I'll make it better."

He pulled his penis out of her hand. "No," she said, and she twisted to try to take hold of him again.

He avoided her grasp and moved down to settle between her legs. She propped herself on one elbow and took him by the arm, trying to urge him up again. He bit the heel of her hand in a quick stinging nip. "Stop that."

"You won't listen," she gasped. "Get back here already."

He growled. "Don't make me pin you down."

Wait, did she hear that right?

They both froze. He looked unutterably gorgeous, unapologetic, mischievous and half feral, poised as he was with his broad shoulders between her thighs. Stunned passion pulsed and she blazed with heat all over again.

She said, "You better not."

His eyes narrowed. He looked down her body and licked his lips. "Or what?"

It could have been a fun game to play but then her hungry clitoris throbbed so hard her knees drew up in reaction, and she lost all composure. She whimpered, "I don't know."

His hands snaked out, faster than sight. He gripped her by the insides of her knees and yanked her legs as wide as they could go. The shock of the movement, the sense of extreme vulnerability, was such that she emitted a shaking groan.

Then his head dove down. He put his mouth on her and she went downright nuclear. He licked and suckled at the stiff little nubbin cloaked by the folds of her private flesh. His mouth was so sure and confident, so urgent yet gentle, that her knees tried to draw up again, but those big hard hands of his encompassed her knees and held her wide open for his ravishment.

The pleasure was insane. It was too much to take. She flung out her hands in a blind search for something, anything to hold on to as he drove her body into a sharp crescendo. She felt the climax roaring toward her and then it slammed into her body with such intensity her torso arched off the floor and noise broke out of her, a high, thin, out-of-control scream of incredulity.

He held his mouth on her, steady and hot, his pale gaze drinking her in as his tongue massaged every last pulse of pleasure out of her, and the sight of him working her with such patient, sensual intent hurtled her into another one. She flew into it, hotter and harder than before, and the tendons in her neck distended as she tried to scream again but she had flown so high the air was too thin, and she couldn't get in a breath to make any noise.

And all the time, he was whispering inside her head. *Beautiful, sweetheart. You're so beautiful. God, you're the most beautiful thing I've ever seen. I want to see you do it again.*

I can't! I-it's too much—Gideon, PLEASE—

Then she lost the words for even telepathy. She held out both hands to him in mute entreaty. And his control broke.

He lunged up to her, guiding the head of his thick penis to her entrance with one hand even as he kissed her, his lips hard and urgent. His mouth was slick with her pleasure. She tasted him, tasted herself. An animal sound came out of her.

She was already climaxing again, her interior muscles rippling, as he slid into her all the way to the hilt, and it was so fucking perfect, she was so fucking perfect, he went on a hopscotch skip straight into the land of crazy.

He poured his own climax into her welcoming body, a helpless shuddering gush. But it wasn't enough, it wasn't even close to enough, it only fed his hunger. A deep growl broke from his chest. He took her by the wrists and pinned her down, and he drove into her in hard, pounding strokes, as she ate eagerly at his mouth and met every thrust of his hips with hers. He came again, and again, and each time she came with him, until at last she lay limp underneath him and he had no more to spend.

He might have slept, hands loosely clasped on her wrists. He wasn't sure. At some point he roused to awareness enough to mutter, "Too heavy?"

His penis had softened but he was still inside her, and it was so gorgeous she didn't want to lose the sensation. His head was pillowed in her hair. She couldn't move her head. She couldn't even open her eyes. She made a herculean effort to respond and managed, "Huh uh."

His body moved in a big sigh. She could feel his pulse, strong and slow, against her breastbone. There was another time of formless drifting. Then he said, his voice gravelly with sleep, "Soon as the weather clears, I'm moving in."

He didn't ask, he stated. She probably should have a problem with that. Nah, she was too tired. But she did notice he held very still, as he listened for her response.

She thought she might have rug burn, and her nose itched. She slipped one of her wrists out of his lax hold so she could scratch it as she yawned. "You'd better. But we're going to have to have a talk about how chatty you get after sex."

Torso to torso as they were, she felt his stomach muscles clench as he burst out laughing. The husky, low sound was as gorgeous as the rest of him. He lifted his head off her hair enough so she could turn to nuzzle at him, and he covered her mouth with his in a quick, physical response. She adored how affectionate he was with her. She adored everything about him. They were going to fight and discover each other's less attractive traits, and the thought of him moving in was frankly rather scary, but there was simply no other alternative. There hadn't been from the moment they both acknowledged the mating shift, so she thought she might as well just go ahead and accept the changes and enjoy the ride, because it was going to be wonderful to wake up in the mornings with him in her bed, to go to sleep at night with him in her body.

Something buzzed nearby.

What was that? She didn't have anything in the living room that buzzed. It buzzed again and Gideon lifted himself away from her body. His expression was still heavy lidded with sensuality but his gaze had turned sharp and alert. He twisted to reach for his cell phone.

He clicked it on. "Yeah."

She watched his face grow cold and still as he listened to the deep, growly voice on the other end. Her sleepy, wondering pleasure vanished in a clench of dread.

"What do you want me to do?" he asked. "I can bring Alice in. She would be safe at HQ and I could help with the search."

She concentrated on the voice on the other end. A male said, "No point in doing that, son. I got plenty of people on the hunt. Just wanted to give you an update. If he's got 'em, all he needs is one more now."

"What about protection on the others?" Gideon asked.

The voice said, "I dispatched the first detail soon after we last talked and told them to keep a low profile so they didn't freak anybody out any more than they already were. We're working as goddamn fast as we can."

She felt sickened. Oh no. *No*.

She had turned cold without his body heat and she felt vulnerable without her glasses on. She put them on and reached for the tangled pile of blanket to pull it around her as Gideon set the phone aside. He turned to her, the expression in his eyes grave.

"What's happened?"

"Bayne got confirmation from the airlines," Gideon told her. He reached out and picked her up, blanket and all, and cradled her against his chest. "The three chameleons scheduled to fly to L.A. never made it to check-in. Their seats were given last minute to three people waiting to fly standby. I know you know them, sweetheart. They're—"

"Stewart Rogers. His mom, Leigh. Her fiancé, Jim Welch," she whispered. She thought of the delicately boned boy, his sweet little earnest face, those serious eyes behind Coke-bottle-thick spectacles and his shy, rare smile. He took after his mother, a gentle, kind woman. Something roared in her ears. "Stewie's in my class, Gideon. Not Stewie. Please don't tell me that."

He held her with his entire big body. He threw off heat like a furnace but it still wasn't enough to drive away the killing cold.

"Sweetheart, I would give anything in the world," Gideon said, "to be able to not tell you that."

Somewhere outside, she could have sworn she heard the wicked wind laugh.

Chapter Seven

Love

S he got to her feet, anxious to do something, anything, to push the news away. Gideon rose to stand beside her. He rubbed her back as he asked, "Can you think of anything Stewart or his mother might have said in the last few days that might have seemed different or out of place?"

He sounded so calm she wanted to scream at him. Stewart and Leigh might have been murdered in the most horrible way even as she and Gideon had been making love. She put both hands over her mouth, shaking with the effort to find some kind of control.

"Remember, Alice, we don't know what happened to them," he said. Rogers and Welch were pretty far down on the alphabet. If the killer had taken them, he might hold on to them until he had his seventh sacrifice. "The only thing we know is that they're missing. They may not be dead."

She looked up to find Gideon watching her closely. There was pain in his eyes. Even though he didn't know any of the people, he was hurting too, hurting for her. The sight clicked her back into balance. "Give me a minute," she said, "I need to calm down so I can concentrate."

He nodded. "I'll make us some coffee."

He walked into the kitchen, and some other time she was going to remember with relish the sight of his nude figure moving around her apartment with total confidence. For now she simply scooped up the blanket and her shredded nightgown and took them to her bedroom to dump on the bed. Even though it was still full dark outside, the illuminated clock on her bedside table read 7:08 AM. She felt she was marking the time's passing with each dark event and she would never forget the numbers. Nightmare, 3:23. Missing friends, 7:08.

She took a quick two-minute shower to sluice off the evidence of their mating, ran her toothbrush over her teeth, then she dressed in the soft, comfortable clothes she had worn the night before. By the time she had finished, she was able to think again.

She walked into the kitchen. Gideon had slipped on his jeans but remained barefoot and bare-chested. The coffee had finished brewing, and he had already poured two cups. He handed one to her with a quick kiss, the short stubble from his unshaven face scraping her chin. "I make it strong," he warned.

"That's okay, I need strong right now," she said. She brought the cup to her lips and sipped. The black, pungent brew was like a kick in the teeth. That was a good thing. She cleared her throat. "I'm just going to talk, like I did last night. Okay?"

"Okay," he said. He leaned back against the counter, drank coffee and watched her.

"Stewie was so excited to be going to see his grandma and grandpa. They can't afford to make the trip very often, so this visit was a big deal. He had his backpack packed by Wednesday. His mom lets him carry whatever toys and books he wants in his carry-on so he has things to keep him busy on the flight. Leigh and Jim had just gotten engaged. They were going to break the news to Leigh's parents once they got to California."

"They're on a tight budget?" Gideon asked. She nodded. "How does Leigh afford private schooling for Stewart? Or is that why their budget is so tight?"

"I think Leigh said once that her parents help with the tuition," she said. She drank more of the bitter brew and kept going. Now that she had started talking, she didn't seem able to stop. "And I'm sure they qualify for a hardship scholarship, which would reduce the fees. In the group we all help each other out as we can, you know, according to the situation and what the other person will accept. Free babysitting or whatever. Sometimes we barter. Leigh was pretty thrilled to get a ride to JFK airport instead of having to pay for a shuttle…"

Her voice trailed away. Gideon's coffee cup came down on the counter. He asked calmly, "Do you know who was supposed to give them a ride?"

She shook her head. "I know Alex offered," she said. "I did too. I don't know if anybody else did or whose offer they accepted."

"Okay," he said. "We need to talk to Schaffer and everybody else to see if we can pinpoint who saw them last." He spoke over his shoulder as he turned away. "I'm going to jump in the shower really quick. Sweetheart, do you mind going to the station with me for a while?"

"Not at all," she said. She stared after him as he strode out of the room. As they had talked, his Power had spiked, sharp and sulfurous, even as his face and demeanor remained soldier-calm. She had said something that interested him, maybe interested him a lot, but he hadn't seen fit to share whatever it was with her.

Her feelings weren't hurt. She was willing to wait and find out why he had shut down.

She just wanted to know what it was she had said.

Gideon scooped up his pile of stuff—gun, clothes, toiletry bag and phone. Moving fast, he hit the bathroom, shut the door and turned on the shower. Soon as the sound of the water filled the room, he hit Bayne on speed dial.

Bayne answered on the first ring. "What's up?"

Gideon asked, "Where's Schaffer?"

"Alex Schaffer? Last I heard, his guards reported him moving around inside his townhouse, safe and sound. All the chameleons are at home, except for the three missing and the ones who we've confirmed have made it to Arizona. Why?"

"I don't know," he growled. "He just keeps coming up in conversation. It's piqued my interest." He told

Bayne rapidly about the conversation with Alice. "All the chameleons need to be questioned again. Alice said Schaffer offered Welch and the Rogers a ride to the airport. She did too, but we know she didn't take them."

Bayne swore. "We've been calling all the limo services to see if the Rogers had booked a trip with one of them."

Holding his cell to his ear with one hand, Gideon unfastened his jeans with the other and jerked them off. Sixty-second shower, no shave. He and Alice could hit the door in under five minutes. He said to Bayne, "We've been focused on the chameleons as the victims. Thing is, one of them might also be the killer."

Alice pushed the living room furniture back into place. She straightened the coffee table in front of the couch. Someone knocked on the front door, a quiet, tentative tap that had her nearly leaping out of her skin.

Her heart still knocking hard, she moved to flip on the outside light and peer through the keyhole.

Alex stood outside in a black wool coat and muffler, hands under his arms and his shoulders hunched against the whip of wind, snow and ice. He was a quiet, unassuming-looking man in his early sixties, with receding gray hair. Usually he was meticulously groomed, but now he looked haggard and so miserable, she found herself unlocking and opening the door.

She said, "Alex, what on earth are you doing here?"

He gave her a sad look as he said, "I didn't wake you, did I? I have been fretting about you all night. I finally had to come see if you were all right."

"For heaven's sake, come in." She stepped back and opened the door wide.

Alex ducked his head and stepped forward. The wind blasted down the steps and into the opening. It brought with it a whip of snow and outside scent—

—and a faint chemical taint…but no scent at all from Alex.

All her thoughts flatlined as she stumbled back. Stupidly, she tried to close the door again.

And Alex's step turned into a lunge as he brought his gloved hands out from underneath his arms. A glint of light came off a long, thin knife he gripped in one hand, while he slammed the door wide open with the other.

"Oh gods," she said.

Alex's sad gaze had turned bright with a fanatical light. He said, "Yes, Alice, oh *gods*. And Abraham said to the Lord, 'Behold, here I am.' It is the most holy sacrifice to give the gods those you love. And the Lord said, 'In blessing I will bless thee, and in multiplying I will multiply thy seed as the stars of the heaven'…"

She flung out a hand, grabbed hold of something, screamed, "*You crazy murdering bastard!*"

Nearby, there was a smash of splintering wood.

Alex had brought his knife hand back for a killing blow. "Only show me your will, gods, as I give to you another one of my own…"

She flung what she had grabbed at him. It was a small potted plant. The pot hit Alex in the chest with a spray of dirt. He flinched and grabbed for her throat. The knife arched—

A silent behemoth hit Alex with a body slam that sent the smaller man crashing to the ground. At the same time, Alice was knocked back with a flattened hand shoved into her chest. She lost her balance, fell and scuttled away from the doorway with her head ducked.

Everything went still. She dared to look behind her.

Alex lay on his back. His throat was torn out, his knife hand crushed beyond recognition.

The monster from Haley's apartment crouched over the body. The planes and angles of his face and body were all wrong. There was one difference: this time he was quite nude and dripping wet.

He bared his teeth, icy gaze alight with incredulous fury. "You opened your front door to him?"

Alice threw up her hands and cried, "He was my boss!"

Her cry turned into a sob, and suddenly the monster became Gideon again. He dove forward, grabbed her and clenched her to his chest. She buried her face in his hot, wet skin. He was breathing hard, a fine tremor rippling through his muscles.

Gideon said grimly, "Well, he's not anymore."

The time came around again for the annual Festival of the Masque, where all creatures, Elder Races or gods, pay homage to the dance that drives and sustains the universe. Planets swirl around their suns, galaxies spin in space. Even tiny atoms joined in the movement.

Every winter solstice, Cuelebre Tower put on one of the most lavish spectacles in the world, complete with a horde of paparazzi and a red carpet. Celebrities and dignitaries from humankind and all the Elder Races attended. A crowd of two thousand attendees wore extraordinary, designer jeweled costumes and masks that glittered with onyx and diamonds. Cuelebre's public hall was decorated with great swathes of ivory and gold cloth, towering ice sculptures, and champagne flowed like water.

A traditional Masque officially began with a procession of the gods and ended with everyone unmasking at midnight, although most of the parties continued till dawn. Most gatherings had volunteers dress up to play the part of the gods. Usually at the school fundraiser, the gods were played by the school trustees. Here, she had no doubt that the procession of the gods would be an elaborate affair played by professional actors.

Alice stared at everything and everyone with wide eyes. Now and then, she caught glimpses across the hall of Dragos Cuelebre, Lord of the Wyr, and his beautiful new mate. In that striking way that mated Wyr had, they moved in sync together, always aware of where the other one was. Alice and Gideon would develop the same ability over time.

At first Alice had been reluctant to come to the Tower Masque. Along with the rest of her community, she was grieving for her friends who had died the week before, and still in shock from discovering Alex Schaffer had been responsible for the murder of ten chameleons. In light of recent events, Broadway Elementary had canceled its annual fundraiser as the school trustees struggled to regroup and look for new leadership.

But Gideon had gotten two tickets to the Tower Masque at a time when no one could beg, borrow or steal them. He had coaxed, and she had capitulated, and now she was glad she had come just to witness the sheer spectacle of the event. They had made a pact to stay until the unmasking at midnight. It was their first official date.

After catching a glimpse of all the extravagant finery in the hall, she felt self-conscious, having worn a simple black sheath dress, high-heeled, peep-toed black patent leather pumps, and a plain black satin half-mask. She had bought contact lenses just for the occasion.

She tugged at her slim skirt. She hoped she didn't look too plain. As if he had read her mind, Gideon bent his head to say in her ear, "You are the most elegant and stunning woman present."

She turned to give him a startled grin. His icy pale gaze met and held hers with a private smile. Clad in a sleek black tux and a plain black half-mask that matched hers, he was so lethally sexy she could hardly believe he was hers. "I just hope I'm doing my handsome escort justice."

Her escort, her mate. The wonder of it stilled her breath.

He tugged at one of her corkscrew curls and released it, watching as it sprang back into place. He never seemed to tire of doing that. She didn't have the heart to tell him how much it irritated her. He whispered, "I couldn't be more proud to be your mate."

The crowd fell away, and it was just the two of them. She reached up to touch the corner of his straight, sexy mouth, and whispered back, "Me, too."

Then suddenly they were no longer alone. A brawny, tanned giant of a male had joined them. It was Gideon's boss, Bayne. As Alice turned with Gideon to face the newcomer, she drew in a deep breath to brace herself against the impact of his presence. Like all immortal Wyr, Bayne radiated a ferocious energy. He hadn't bothered with a mask, had already removed his tie, and his dress shirt was open at the throat.

Bayne said to Gideon, "The hell's the matter with you, son? Go grab your mate a glass of champagne and some of those fancy-ass hors d'oeuvres before they're all gone."

Gideon met her gaze. He smiled. "I'll be right back."

"Thank you," she said.

"My pleasure, sweetheart."

He turned to Bayne, who said, "You better hurry. The procession is about to start. I'll stay with her while you're gone."

They both watched Gideon wind his way through the crowd toward the refreshments. Then Bayne turned to her. "Good to see you, Alice. I'm glad you two decided to use the tickets. How are you doing?"

Bayne had given the tickets to Gideon? "It was a lovely gift," she said. "I'm doing much better, thanks."

To say she had not been at her best when she first met the gryphon was putting it mildly. She had held it together when she had really looked at Alex, the knife lying on the floor beside his sprawled form. After holding her so tightly he left bruises, Gideon had covered Alex's face and shoulders with his bath towel, gone to dress and made phone calls. Alice had taken a seat at one end of her couch and remained calm and still when Bayne had arrived shortly after, questioned them both, and supervised the removal of the body. Then she had taken one look at the deep red pool of blood that had soaked into the carpet by her front door and slid into a complete meltdown.

Gideon had snatched her up and carried her out of the room, his face tight. She wasn't sure who was responsible, but despite the blizzard and it being a Saturday before a major holiday, she'd had new carpet installed within the hour.

Now her cheeks darkened at the memory. She said to the sentinel towering beside her, "I'm sorry about how we first met."

"I am, too," Bayne said. He glanced down at her, regret in his rugged features. "I wish we had been able to catch the fucker before he got to you."

She sent him a sidelong glance. "That wasn't what I meant."

The gryphon stood at ease. As he rested his hands on his hips, his jacket parted to reveal a glimpse of his two gun holsters. In the last week, with Gideon moving in, and his friends from both the WDVC and the army dropping by with the casual air of those hoping to be fed, Alice was growing used to the sight of large muscular people wandering around armed. She and Gideon had also bought a larger fridge and a larger dish set.

"I know what you meant," said Bayne. "You found your friend murdered, discovered your mate and caught a killer, all in less than eighteen hours. To top it all off, the killer was someone you knew and had trusted for years. You think you weren't entitled to throw a little bit of a fit?"

She chuckled. "Well, when you put it like that." Then she sobered. "I keep trying to make sense of what Alex was saying at the end, and I can't. I think he was quoting the Bible, of all things."

"Don't waste your energy on trying to make sense of it," said Bayne. "If you'll excuse my language, the dude was effing nuts. You wouldn't believe what we found in the basement of his townhouse. He had made plans to start up the True Colors support group before he ever took that first trip down to Jacksonville seven years ago. He had books and scribblings from all the major religions, and prayers painted on the walls and ceilings. He'd added up and subtracted all kinds of numbers that told him the pope was the fricking antichrist. He had this whole messianic delusion going on, about repopulating the Earth with chameleon Wyr after he had sacrificed what he most loved to the gods—his people. He planned to keep on killing until he had gotten some kind of divine sign. I'm telling you—Whack. O."

They had found more than books and scribbling in the basement. Stewart, his mother Leigh, and Jim Welch had been found bound and gagged, but alive. Alex's guards had been looking to keep a killer out of his house, not to keep Alex inside. He had given them the slip by going out his back gate when he had come after Alice. If he had not been quite so obsessed with form and ritual, Stewie and his family wouldn't have survived. As it was, he had told them once he had sacrificed Alice, he would be able to kill the rest of them over the next several days. Leigh told Alice, in a phone call several days later, that Alex had seemed astonished at their distress. He couldn't understand why they weren't aware of the honor he was bestowing upon them.

"It's all so hard to believe," Alice whispered. She shuddered and rubbed her bare arms. Alex had always been a little tight-assed, a little too buttoned up, but no one had ever conceived of him as being anything other than normal.

"Well, hell," said the gryphon. He regarded her with chagrin. "Gideon's gonna shoot me. This was supposed to be your night out for fun, and here I've got you looking like you've seen a ghost."

"It's all right," she told him. "Talking it through is much better than trying to ignore it. It's just going to take a while to process."

She spotted Gideon's light blond head over the crowd. He was working his way back to them. The joy she felt as she watched him approach was almost too much for her body to contain.

Bayne had also turned and caught sight of Gideon. The gryphon told her in a quiet voice, "We all think very highly of him. He's one of the finest men I know."

Her eyes fixed on her mate, Alice said, "He's one of the finest men I know, too."

At last Gideon reached them. He presented her with a plate piled high with delicacies and petit fours. In his other hand he cradled two glasses of champagne. "Sorry," he said to Bayne as Alice took one of the glasses from him. "I didn't think I could juggle three glasses without dropping something."

"S'all right," said Bayne. "Champagne's not my drink."

Gideon gave Alice a swift kiss. "What were you two talking about while I was gone?"

She and the gryphon looked at each other. "Mating," she said. "And how fast it can hit."

"I blame it on the air," said Gideon. He winked at her. "There's an awful lot of Wyr mating pheromones floating around these days."

"Well, you both look very happy, so good on you," said Bayne, with a hearty clap to Gideon's shoulders that threatened the plate of food. "As for me, I just might start wearing a gas mask."

At that moment, the crowd parted and the procession of the gods started. They were led by the god Taliesin who was portrayed this year by a slender male. Taliesin was followed in short order by the other gods, each sumptuously costumed, and the crowd in the hall swept into a low bow as they passed.

Alice couldn't help but shiver as Azrael, the god of death, drew near. Old legends told that a god attended every Masque. If there were ever a time when death might appear, she thought, it would be at this Masque.

The elegant, glittering figure passed by. She sucked in a breath and called herself silly. The last in the procession was the goddess of love, Inanna. The tall, striking woman moved with regal sinuousness, a wild mane of waist-length blonde hair flowing back from a feline mask. Her gown had seven embroidered lions pulling seven chariots. As Inanna drew level, the goddess turned to look at them, almost as if she had heard Bayne speak. Alice thought she caught a glimpse of something vast and amused gazing at the gryphon out of the mask's eyeholes. Alice shook her head sharply, and the strange vision passed.

Then the orchestra struck the first notes, all the participants took their places, and the dance began.

Natural Evil

Dedication

To my editor, Heather, and to Amy, and my
fabulous cover artist Angela Waters. Thank you
all for your championship, talent and hard
work!

And especially to you, the readers.

Chapter One

The Depths

Claudia couldn't tell that the sizable lump on the highway shoulder was a body. Not at first.

She was traveling 110 mph on I-80W through a solitary stretch of Nevada. Sage, silvery tan, gold and light brown, splashed across the expanse of desert ringed by snow-covered dark mountains. The pale sky mirrored the land with great swathes of silver-lined gray clouds. The windswept silence was immense as ferocious heat boiled off the pavement and radiated from the afternoon's piercing yellow-white sun. She had heard it said that the desert spaces of the world were where the Djinn came to dance.

Afterwards, she never could say why she'd stopped to investigate. She'd simply obeyed an impulse, slammed on the brakes and reversed. No other vehicles were visible on either side of the highway, and she was the only thing alive. Or so she'd thought.

Her 1984 BMW came even with the lump. Her heart sank as she stared at it. It was some sort of canine, an unusually large one. Not that she was any judge of breed, but it had to be a domestic animal. It certainly wasn't a wolf or a coyote. The body was muscular, with a large, powerful chest and a long, heavy bone structure that was still graceful, and a wide, well-proportioned head. The dog had taken some horrific damage. Its neck was thick and swollen, and its dark brown and black coat scored with large raw patches.

She wondered what it was doing in the middle of the desert, if it had been hit or if it had been traveling unsecured in the back of a truck and fallen out. Possibly both. She hoped it had died fast.

One of its huge front paws twitched.

She slammed the BMW into park and grabbed her water bottle before her brain caught up with her actions. As she lunged out of the car, she shed the insulation she had worked so hard to acquire, shifting through an invisible barrier to fully enter into and connect with her surroundings.

She fell to her knees beside the dog. Hell, forget unusually large—it was freakishly massive. She might not know much about dogs, but she knew few breeds reached that size. Bigger than a German shepherd, too heavy for a Great Dane, it had to be some kind of mastiff. Damn, it was not only alive, but it looked like it might be conscious. It was panting fast and shallow, muzzle open and tongue lolling. Its eyes were closed, the surrounding muscles around the eye sockets tense with suffering.

"Good Christ," she said. The wind roared through miles of solitude and snapped away the words.

She eased a hand under the dog's head, lifted it and tried to trickle a small amount of water into its mouth. It had a set of wicked chompers, white, strong teeth as long as her fingers. Hard to tell if it noticed or reacted to the water. She thought not.

Claudia was a bit taller than the average woman, with a weight that fluctuated between 140 and 145 pounds. The dog was easily half again her size, perhaps 200 or even 220. No normal human woman could hope to lift that kind of dead weight into the back seat of her car, but Claudia was not quite a normal human woman.

She had a Power that manifested as telekinetic ability, but it was just a spark, so she had to be touching whatever she chose to use it on. She could manage a bit of telepathy if someone was standing close enough to her, and her spark might be enough for her to travel to an Other land, one of those magic-filled places that had formed when time and space had buckled at the Earth's formation. Might or might not. She didn't know. She'd never tried.

As far as Power or magical ability went, her telekinesis wasn't much, but it did allow her to do a few interesting things. For one thing, she might be able to boost her lifting capacity enough so that she could get the dog into the back seat. Unfortunately, its injuries were so severe, she would probably kill it when she tried to move it.

She thought of her .40 caliber Glock. The gun was stored in the trunk of her car along with her suitcases and camping gear. She never underestimated the impact of a single, well-aimed bullet, for good or ill. *One shot, one kill*, as the sniper in her unit used to say. In this case, it would be a mercy to put the dog out of his misery. Death had to be better than this slow, solitary expiration in the desert.

Putting him down might be a mercy but everything inside her rebelled at the thought. She set her jaw. If the dog didn't die, she would get it—she glanced down the dog's body and discovered that not only was he male, but he hadn't been neutered—she would get him some help.

Once she made the decision, she moved fast. She dug through the canvas bags of camping supplies in her trunk until she located the ground tarp. Refolding the plastic into a smaller size that the dog could still fit on, she left enough room to grasp the edges. Then she laid the tarp on the ground beside the animal.

The next ten minutes felt like enduring a two-year tour of duty. The dog's suffering was a gravity well that held her anchored to its wretchedness. The wind blasted the bare skin of her arms and face with tiny stinging grains of the scorching pale sand. The sand had crusted the raw edges of the dog's wounds, until she moved him and the wounds reopened. They bled brilliant, glistening crimson that trickled through the pale ivory-gold of the crusted sand. Normally the two colors looked lovely together.

She talked to the dog, random words of encouragement, and she exercised her extensive vocabulary of swear words as she strained her leg and back muscles along with her telekinesis. At last, she managed to shift him onto the tarp and then into the back seat.

During the worst of it, the dog opened his eyes and looked at her. The intelligence and the bright pain in his eyes were twin spears that shoved into her heart. When she finally slid into the driver's seat again, she had to clean off her hands and wipe at her own wet eyes before she could see enough to start the engine.

The dog didn't die.

Less than two minutes later a county patrol car swooped up behind her, lights flashing.

She pulled onto the shoulder and parked, rolled down her window, moved her Ray-Bans to the top of her head and watched as a gray-haired man in a short-sleeved, tan uniform walked up to her car. His bladed, smiling face was lined with good humor and friendliness. He braced a hand on her door.

"Lady, that's some well-maintained engine you've got under this hood," he said. "I tagged you at one twenty-five."

She handed him her New York driver's license and registration. The license photo was of a lean, fit forty-year-old woman, with straight ash-blonde, shoulder-length hair, green eyes, spare features and a somewhat crooked nose. She had broken it once in Kandahar. He glanced from the license to her, verifying her identity.

She said, "As you can see, I'm not from around here, and I've got a badly injured dog in the back seat. Can you direct me to the nearest animal hospital or vet—or better yet, could you show me and write the ticket afterward?"

The man's quick, dark gaze shot to the back seat. She watched his expression change. "That your animal?"

She shook her head. "Found him by the road a few miles back."

He glanced at her dirt- and blood-smeared T-shirt and cargo pants. "You got him in the car all by yourself?"

"Yeah."

"How did you manage that?"

The skin around her mouth tightened. "Adrenaline, I guess."

His grave gaze met hers. "Might be kindest if I put him down."

His hand had moved to rest on his firearm. Something inside her went cold and still as she tracked the movement out of the corner of her eye. Her hands clenched on the steering wheel. In retrospect, storing her gun in the trunk of her car had been a stupid thing to do.

"Might be," she said. She kept her tone soft and even. Nonaggressive. "I had that thought myself. But it wouldn't be fair. He's endured a lot to get this far. And even though he was awake, he didn't bite me when I got him in the car. I'm going to give him a fighting chance. Don't tell me there's no vet for a hundred miles."

A decision wavered between them, invisible like a heat wave rising off the pavement. She moved her left hand to her thigh and clenched it into a fist as she tracked his resting on his gun.

The trooper tucked her license and registration into his shirt pocket and straightened. "There's a vet nearby. Follow me."

That was how Claudia and the dog got a police escort into Nirvana, Nevada, population 1,611.

The town was located in the foothills of a small mountain range, its streets laid out in a simple north/south, east/west grid system. She followed close behind the sheriff's patrol car. He sped through the quiet neighborhood streets and pulled to a stop in front of a ranch-style house that had a screened-in front porch that faced west. A dusty Dodge Ram pickup was parked in the driveway.

She placed the sheriff in the latter half of his fifties, but he was a fit man who could move fast enough if the situation warranted it. Even as she parked behind him, he was out of his patrol car and striding toward her BMW.

She set her sunglasses on top of her head again and slid out of the car to join him. They considered the grim mess in the back seat.

The sheriff took a breath. Rodriguez, his name tag said. "We really should have the vet put him down. One quick injection and he wouldn't feel any more pain."

She kept her expression noncommittal as she nodded. "He's made it this far," she said. "So I think not. Can you grab one end of the tarp while I pull him out?"

He sighed and nodded. Together they used the tarp as a stretcher. She glanced up as they carried the dog to the house. A man had come to the front door when they'd parked. He held the screen door open for them. As they approached, she caught a glimpse of a weathered face under an equally weathered cowboy hat. He was older than the sheriff by at least ten years. The sprinkle of hair showing underneath the cowboy hat was white.

The man said to Rodriguez, "Kitchen table."

The sheriff blew out a breath and nodded. They went into the house, through a living room filled with large, worn furniture and piled with books, down a short hallway into a kitchen that was stocked with a couple of old refrigerators, white-painted cabinets, scarred Formica countertops and a worn linoleum floor. The floor felt uneven under her footsteps. She glanced down. There was a metal drain in the floor near the back door. The kitchen had a pervasive odor of disinfectant. It was probably perfectly clean, as the scent suggested, but she still wouldn't be comfortable accepting an invitation to eat a meal in it.

The kitchen table was metal and bordered by picnic-style benches with a chair at each end. They eased the dog onto the table. The man in the cowboy hat pushed past them. She watched his battered profile grow intent. He pulled a pair of latex gloves out of a drawer and said, "Move the benches and chairs into the hall, John."

"You got it."

She stepped into a corner as the sheriff pulled furniture out of the way.

She kept an eye on the sheriff as she said to Cowboy Hat, "This is my dog. I'm paying his vet bill, and I want you to do everything you can to save him."

Rodriguez paused. His stillness lasted only a heartbeat. She would have missed it if she hadn't been watching him.

She turned back to Cowboy Hat. He had raised bushy, white eyebrows.

Rodriguez moved the last bench aside as he said, "This is Doc Dan Jackson. He's the only vet within sixty miles."

"People kept knocking on my door with their injured pets," said Johnson. "Gave up trying to retire seven years ago."

"Dan, this is Claudia Hunter. Says she found the dog on I-80."

It was her turn to raise her eyebrows. Rodriguez didn't have to pull out her driver's license in order to introduce her by name. Showed he was paying attention. The vet unlocked the cabinet and withdrew vials of clear liquid and a syringe.

She moved. When the vet turned, she was standing between him and the dog on the table. She met the sharp inquiry in his eyes with her own clear gaze. "Doesn't matter if I haven't had him long. He is my dog now." She looked down at the vials he held in his gnarled hands. She repeated, "I want you to do everything you can to save him."

Jackson opened his hands to show her what he held, turning the vials so she could read the labels. He said, "Your new dog needs to be anesthetized so I can work on him. I'm going to sedate him with a combination of Valium and ketamine so that I can insert an endotracheal tube and administer Isoflurane, which is a gas anesthetic. Then I'm going to try to save his life. That okay by you?"

"Yes," she said.

"Then get the hell out of my way," he said.

She stepped back, watching closely as he administered the injections. Maybe it was her imagination, but it seemed the dog eased and began breathing easier almost immediately. The vet gave her a scowling look. "Get the hell out of my kitchen too."

"I want to help," she said.

Jackson moved quickly to insert a tube down the dog's throat. "You a vet tech?"

"Nope," she said.

"An EMT? Human nurse? Any goddamn thing that might be useful?"

"My unit got shot up a couple times in Afghanistan," she said. "Once we had to deal with the aftermath of a roadside bomb. I've triaged more than my share of wounds and sometimes they were ugly. I didn't bandage animals, and I wasn't a medic. But if you need an extra pair of steady hands from someone who won't faint at the sight of blood, I can provide it."

Jackson snorted without looking up from his work, but after a moment he said, "Grab a pair of gloves. Top drawer on your left."

She opened the drawer, pulled out a pair of latex gloves and yanked them on.

Rodriguez folded his arms as he watched the exchange. His original friendly expression had morphed into a scowl. He said, "Isn't that against the law, Dan? You could lose your license."

"Don't be stupid," said the vet. "I'm not letting her actually do anything surgical on the animal, and you're not the veterinarian State Board. Like she said, an extra pair of steady hands. Speaking of which, hold this a sec." He thrust an implement at her.

She looked at it with interest. It was kind of like a scalpel, nice and sharp on one end. It would make a good hand-to-hand weapon.

"I have questions I want to ask you," Rodriguez said to her.

"So ask," she said. She stood balanced on the balls of her feet and kept her eyes on the vet as she held the implement in one hand and flipped it, then flipped it again.

As she twirled the implement between her fingers, Jackson glanced sidelong at her. He said irritably, "Stop that."

She stopped and stood quietly as she watched him inspect the dog. He probed the dog's swollen neck, and his face tightened. He held out his hand and she handed the implement back to him. "Still has rope tied around his neck," he said. "Get your fingers over here. Keep his skin pulled back so I can cut the rope off."

"Shit." She bent over and pulled the swollen, abraded flesh apart as best she could.

"Can you take me back to where you found the dog?" Rodriguez asked.

"Nope," she said.

"That's a pretty glib response," said the sheriff. "You actually give your answer any thought?"

"I'm from New York," she said tersely, sparing the sheriff a single sharp look. "I'm not familiar with this area. The desert all looks the same to me, and I wasn't paying attention to where I was when I decided to stop to investigate the lump beside the road."

"First you say you found the dog," Rodriguez said. "Now you say he's yours. Animal torture is against the law."

"For God's sake, John!" Jackson snapped.

"Something doesn't add up about her story," Rodriguez said, his voice hard. "There's no damn way she could get an animal of his size and weight into her car all by herself."

She angled her jaw out. Should she tell the sheriff about her telekinesis? She thought over recent events and stuck by her original instinct, remaining silent.

The vet said, "This dog was dragged behind a vehicle before the rope broke. Go check her goddamn bumper. If you find something, arrest her. If not, go away. We've got a lot to do here and it's going to take a while." He lifted one shoulder in a fatalistic shrug. "Unless, of course, the dog dies."

"I've said that a lot in the last forty-five minutes," she said. That dog had one of the strongest wills to live she'd ever seen. She had a feeling he wasn't going to die on Jackson's table. She added to Rodriguez, "If you're going to ticket me, set it on the counter along with my license and registration. I'll pay it before I leave town."

The sheriff was silent for a moment. Then he growled, "Fine."

Rodriguez slammed out the front door. In ten minutes he was back. He slapped papers on the corner of the counter. He said to the vet, "Call me."

Jackson nodded without a break in his work. The sheriff left without another word.

Claudia's stomach was in a knot by the time Jackson finally got the rope cut away from the dog's neck. They washed him next, cleaning him of sand and grit. There were raw wounds all over his body. Jackson's aged face was set, his pale blue eyes burning. She had a feeling she looked the same way. He took X-rays, diagnosed broken ribs and wrapped them, and he had to cut out two bullets. They worked for a long time in a silence that was broken only by Jackson's brusque commands. She did everything he told her to do, and she did it quickly.

Jackson's medicine was mundane, which was to say, he did not use spells in any of his procedures. She didn't sense any sparks of Power on him or anywhere in his house, but then her magic sense was almost nil. Most creatures, items and places felt mundane to her. She'd never bothered to try discovering if her spark of Power was enough to cross over to an Other land because, in part, she couldn't sense the land magic of the crossover passages.

Finally Jackson finished working on the dog. When he removed the endotracheal tube, straightened and stripped off his gloves, she stretched her aching back and shoulders and stripped off hers as well, tossing them into the hazardous-waste bin by the back door.

Jackson opened his battered fridge and pulled out two Heinekens. He popped the tops off the green bottles and handed one to her. Claudia accepted it and took a swallow. She watched him dig into his shirt pocket to pull out a cigarette lighter and a pack of Camels. He offered a cigarette to her. She shook her head. He tapped one out of the box, stuck it between his lips and kicked open the back screen door to step outside. When he held the door open for her, she glanced at the bandaged, unconscious dog.

"He won't be waking up for a few hours," said Jackson. His pale blue eyes were keen.

She took a deep breath and stepped outside after him. She drank her Heineken and looked around the scene as Jackson smoked. She could see the back end of the modest row houses that lined the sandy two-lane street. To the north, rising foothills provided an elevated horizon. The brown land was sprinkled with dots of sagebrush, cacti and yucca trees. A few of the houses had small landscaped areas of improbable green.

Jackson's backyard didn't. It was the same brown as the rest of the desert. A small, battered trailer that rested on concrete blocks instead of tires took up most of the space in his yard. Bare concrete steps led up to the trailer's door. The window coverings were raised. The trailer looked uninhabited, the parking space beside it empty.

A large part of the evening sky had darkened. She nodded toward it. "Weird."

Jackson glanced in that direction. "Sandstorm's blowing in. It'll probably hit in another hour. Looks like we'll lose cable again."

She raised her eyebrows. "That happen often?"

"A fair amount. Cell phone reception is spotty here anyway, and it goes out completely in one of these storms. Sometimes we lose the phone lines too. If the phone lines go, it'll take at least a day before we get them back."

"Damn."

"The storm might blow over in a couple of hours, or it might go all night. I knew one once that lasted a couple days, although that's unusual. People watch DVDs, hang out in the bars, and there's always a poker game somewhere." He shrugged. "You get used to it."

The storm didn't look that far off. She guessed it would be blowing in very soon, but for the moment, the heat of the early evening pressed against her skin. Spring hadn't officially arrived yet; the vernal equinox was in just a few days. She liked the summer and winter solstices, and the vernal and autumnal equinoxes. They added a cadence to the year and made it feel balanced.

The heat would go out of the day quickly, especially now that the sun had begun to descend. She imagined the spring nights would get quite cold, but for now she was still comfortable with bare arms.

Jackson finished his cigarette, stubbed it out and tossed the brown butt into a coffee can by his back door.

"I'd say you don't talk much for a girl," he said. "Except you don't talk much, period. Those five words were the most you've said in a couple hours."

She took a pull from her beer. "Ran out of things to say a few years back."

Jackson grunted, tapped out another cigarette and lit it. He drew deeply on the cigarette and with evident pleasure. The glowing coal at the end flared bright red. "Why's that?"

She lifted a shoulder. Too much blood, too much death. Her unit got shot at one too many times, and the last time almost none of them survived to walk away. Sometimes, she thought, things happen that are so bad you go deep inside, down past the point of screaming, into silence.

She finished her Heineken.

Jackson smoked. She liked the smell of the cigarette smoke. It was comforting. It reminded her of people she had cared for more than her own life, people she would never see again this side of death.

He asked, "So what's the real story? You know that dog?"

"Nope," she said. "I found him, just like I said."

He said, "He should've died on that table couple times over."

"I figure," she said. She stretched her neck again, first one way then the other.

"Thought you might," said Jackson. "You know, it could just mean he's one hell of a stubborn dog. I've seen animals with a kind of will to live you wouldn't believe."

"It could." She waited. She thought she knew what might come next.

Jackson did not disappoint. "Or it could mean something else," he said. He pushed his hat back with the tip of his bottle. "Which is why you watched me so damn close the whole time I was working on him, wasn't it? Why you wanted to help. And why you wanted to make sure about the drugs I was giving him. He could just be a stubborn dog that won't die. Or he could be Wyr. In which case, what happened to him wasn't just animal cruelty but attempted murder."

"I figure," Claudia said again.

Chapter Two

Hearth

"B ut the healing capabilities of the Wyr are famous," she continued. "Wouldn't we have seen some of his injuries heal by now?"

"Maybe we did, which is why he didn't die. You don't have the magic sense to tell whether he's Wyr or not," Jackson said. He didn't phrase it as a question.

She answered him anyway. "Nope."

"I don't either. Nor John, or he would have said something."

"Would he?"

"The hell you mean by that?" He aimed a fierce frown in her direction.

Earlier, the vast space she had been driving through had been so empty there hadn't even been a bird visible in the sky. Rodriguez had to have been moving fast just to catch sight of her, let alone catch her on his radar. She knew why she'd been speeding, but she didn't know why he had been. She wondered what had been so urgent it had caused him to drive at such speed. Yet whatever it was, he had abandoned it in order to pull her over.

It could have been coincidence that Rodriguez pulled her over just after she found the dog. The sheriff had only put his hand on his gun, he hadn't drawn it. The dog was so badly injured that anyone might have suggested putting him out of his misery. She'd thought of it herself.

Rodriguez had brought it up twice.

Coincidence and niggles. They were such small things. They almost certainly meant nothing. She kept her tone mild. "Nothing. I don't know the sheriff. I don't know you. That's all."

The vet heaved a sigh. It sounded disgusted. "Well, obviously something happened for you to wonder if the dog might be Wyr."

"Rodriguez brought up a good point," she said. "It wasn't easy getting such a large animal into the back of my car."

"Yeah, but you managed it somehow. So?"

She squinted up at the early evening, storm-swept sky. What was that color? It was not quite orange, not quite red. Maybe that was what brimstone looked like.

"He was awake when I found him," she said. "He was already hurting bad. I hurt him a lot more when I got him in the car." She thought of the look the dog had given her, the sense she had gotten of a sharp intelligence behind the suffering, and searched for more words. They came harder when a body had stopped talking for a time. Jackson was staring at her. Finally she said, "He didn't bite me."

Jackson sighed again. He opened the back screen door and gestured for her to precede him. She moved to the table and he joined her. They both regarded the unconscious dog. Jackson said, "You know, he's probably mundane. He's facing a long, hard recovery, and that's just the physical component of his injuries. After the kind of abuse he's suffered, it might take him months before he trusts anyone again. He's gonna wake up in a few hours. I can keep him medicated for the pain, but I'm still gonna have to crate him."

She pursed her lips. She hated the idea of putting the dog behind bars, especially if he might be Wyr. If he was Wyr, and whoever had tortured him knew it, why had they tried to kill him? What would they do if they found out he wasn't dead? Jackson was sharp but he was also an elderly man, and at the moment the dog couldn't defend himself.

"I should take him instead," she said.

Jackson squinted an eye at her. "And do what? Go where? He's too badly injured to travel, and the storm's blowing in. You said you were from New York. Where are you headed, anyway? You were on I-80 going somewhere, and it won't be good highway driving tonight."

"I'm on vacation," she said. She had walked away from the army four years before she had earned a twenty-year pension, but with what her parents had left her, she got by. She'd been on vacation for the last couple of years, unable to concentrate for long periods of time. Unable to settle into a new job, unable to sleep, unable to stop the nightmares when she did. "I was headed south to do some early camping. But I have no agenda I need to follow. I've got time to look after him."

Like the nearby mountain range, Jackson's profile was worn, the edges softened by age. After a moment he said, "Back trailer's empty."

"Oh yeah?"

"I keep it for my daughter when she comes to visit from Fresno. She's not too comfortable with the layout of my kitchen." She managed to avoid grinning. Jackson continued, "You can stay there to look after the dog, if you like."

"That's generous of you." She couldn't resist and let her fingers stroke lightly over the soft skin of the dog's broad head. It was one of the few places he wasn't covered in gauze. "Might be best if I checked into a motel."

He snorted. "How do you figure? I'm offering you the trailer for free. That's a lot cheaper than a motel room. It has hot and cold running water, propane heat, and it's hooked up to my electricity. The kitchen is small but usable. It's a lot quieter than a motel too, except for the wind, and tonight you're gonna hear that anywhere in Nirvana. And you don't know if that dog's gonna give you any trouble. He should be in an animal hospital, except there isn't one around here. I want to keep him close by for the first night or two, so I can see how he does."

She rubbed the back of her neck. "All right," she said. "That makes sense. Yes, thank you."

"Okay." He paused. "Think we can move him into the trailer while he's still out?"

"If I could wrestle him into my car all by myself, I'm sure that together we can move him into the trailer."

The look he gave her was speculative. Nothing about his mind was worn or softened by age. "I don't believe for a minute that you tortured that dog. You're too angry about what happened to him. But John's right, there's something off about that story. He was in bad enough shape he couldn't help you get him in the car."

She was too many years past innocence to manage a completely innocent smile. But she did bland really well. "I'm stronger than I look."

An hour later, reality had assumed a different appearance. Claudia folded her sleeping bag to use as a bed for the dog, and then she and Jackson carried him into the trailer. She used a surreptitious touch of her telekinesis, which made shifting his massive body more of an inconvenience than a real strain.

Jackson turned on the trailer's heat and showed her how to use the controls. She moved her car to the parking space by the trailer and carried in supplies—her Coleman cooler of food and drinks; the case that held her laptop and satellite phone; the locked metal box that held her stored handgun; the suitcase that contained her clothes, a few paperbacks, and the odd gift of an antique Elder Tarot deck.

As the trailer warmed, the outside cooled fast with the setting of the sun. Inside, the living space was all in miniature, the furnishings a good thirty years old. The kitchen was about as big as a postage stamp. It was possible to wash dishes, cook something on the tiny stove, use the microwave and get something out of the refrigerator without taking a single step. Someone had stocked it with a basic supply of cookware and dishes, and at least the fridge was a decent size.

In the living area, Jackson had folded up the dining table and secured it against the wall, so she could use the L-shaped booth as a couch. An old thirteen-inch television was bolted to a small shelf, along with a VHS tape player and a digital converter box. A portable radio rested on the narrow sill in front of the kitchen sink. The bathroom was almost the size of an airplane's lavatory, except it had the addition of a shower stall. A double-sized mattress rested on a shelf where the trailer was designed to attach to a pickup truck.

She liked the space in the trailer. It was cozy. The shades from the lamps threw a soft, mellow gold over everything. The dog's prone form took up most of the floor space. She set a bowl of water in a corner, near enough so he could reach it, stepping over him carefully as she moved around. She stowed the things from her cooler in the refrigerator, mostly sandwich materials, yogurt, fruit, and bottles of water and unsweetened tea.

After that she showered, dressed in dark jeans, t-shirt and plain black sweatshirt, and slipped on tennis shoes. She found an old set of sheets and blankets in a cupboard and threw them over the mattress, plugged in her satellite cell phone and laptop, and set the old wooden, painted box holding the Tarot deck, along with her books, on the tiny kitchen countertop beside medicinal supplies for the dog.

Then she set the metal case that held her Glock on the booth/couch and sat down beside it. Storing her gun already cleaned and unloaded was an old habit, but to make sure it was in optimum working order, she field-stripped it, racked the slide, reassembled it and snapped a full magazine of ammunition in place. Her movements were fast, sure and automatic. The gun was a familiar companion, as comforting as Jackson's cigarette smoke. Tension eased from her neck and shoulders as she worked.

As a young woman just finishing college, she had watched with deep interest when the Pentagon came close to banning women from active combat in 1994. They had cited both physical and psychological concerns, but the outcry against such a decision had been so public, the Pentagon had been forced to abandon their stance.

None of the seven Elder Races demesnes had ever banned females from any part of their military or ruling structures, so it was viewed as reprehensible for human society in the US to even consider barring women from serving combat duty in the army. The public debate had actually piqued her interest in joining the army. Her abilities had solidified her career path in Special Forces. Two years ago she had retired a Major.

She lived the same story so many other soldiers did. She was haunted by the ghosts of those she had served with who had fallen, by the ghosts of the innocents harmed by war, by the ghosts of decisions she had made and not made, and now would have to live with for the rest of her life.

And there was something that slept deep inside of her that only came awake when she held a gun.

The sound of someone racking a gun slide yanked the dog awake. Adrenaline dumped toxic waste in his bloodstream. He was awash in pain and feral urges. He wanted to tear into flesh. He needed to hear bones break and somebody screaming. He hurt so bad, it almost made him vomit. He breathed shallowly because the binding on his broken ribs wouldn't let him do anything else.

Quiet, warmth, golden light. They made no sense to him. As he worked to get his bearings, a sneakered foot shifted beside his head. The foot was attached to a long, trim, jeans-clad leg. He remembered steel-toed boots slamming into him, and his lips pulled back from his teeth in a silent snarl. If he could have, he would have lunged forward to savage that leg.

That was when he caught scent of her. The woman.

He had been drowning in a dry, fiery ocean of agony, scoured by endless sand and scorched by the sun, when she'd appeared. She'd cradled his head in long, strong fingers, and bathed his parched mouth and throat with cool water.

When he had lost all reason to live, she'd whispered to him, "Don't die."

So he hadn't.

Now they were together in this quiet, warm, golden place. Wherever this was. A knock sounded at the door. He tried to lunge to his feet to protect her, but his abused body wouldn't obey him. He watched through slit eyes as she rose to her feet. She was a long, tall woman who moved with confident, lethal grace. His thirsty soul drank down the sight. Just before she answered the door, she tucked a gun into the waistband of her jeans at the small of her back, underneath her sweatshirt.

She was the one who had racked the slide. If he could have, he would have smiled.

Cold air sliced through the warmth. A worn voice said, "Settling in all right?"

"Yes, thanks," the woman said. "It's cozy in here."

The voice was male. The dog growled. The sound he made was hoarse and broken. Fresh pain erupted in abused throat muscles. The woman turned to stare at him. She said, "Shush."

The calm command in her voice startled him into shushing. But he kept his lips curled, and he showed the newcomer his teeth.

"He's awake," said the other male. "That's a bit early."

"Is it?" the woman said.

The male said, "Doesn't mean anything conclusive. It's just a bit early."

"I understand."

"I'm getting takeout from the diner. It's not fancy but they've got good food. Want me to get supper for you?"

"That'd be great, thanks." The woman dug into her jeans pocket, pulled something out and handed it to the male. "I'll have whatever you're having. Could you buy another meal that has lots of well-cooked beef and hopefully some gravy too? Tomorrow I'll run to the store, but for now I'd like to have something on hand, just in case."

"You got it," the male said.

The blast of cold air cut off as she shut the door.

Now that the other male was gone, the dog's gaze slid out of focus. He started to drift.

The woman came down on her hands and knees in front of his face. "Hey," she said. Her voice was like the rest of her: strong, bright and clean. "My name is Claudia Hunter. Can you talk to me? I'd like you to tell me who you are, and who did this to you."

He ignored her.

She said telepathically, *Cat got your tongue? Come on, say something. Let me know you understand me.*

He closed his eyes.

"Don't have anything to say? You were such a good boy earlier when you didn't bite me. What a sweet, good boy, yes, you are." She paused then crooned, "I think I'm going to name you Precious."

His eyes flared open and shifted toward her in offended startlement.

The woman's own gaze widened. Her eyes were gorgeous. She whispered, "Bloody hell. You *are* Wyr."

So what do you do with a Wyr in his animal form, badly injured, who refuses to talk?

She didn't have a clue. She was making it up as she went along. She turned on her laptop. It cost to have a laptop with satellite communication readiness, along with her sat cell phone, but she had decided the greater connectivity was worth the price in case of emergency. The choice had paid off when she was on the road.

Unfortunately, the weather had a great deal of influence on satellite connectivity. She tried to access the Internet but found she couldn't. Then, without much hope, she tried her sat phone. Same story. And the Wyr wasn't talking for a reason. Maybe that reason was trauma, or maybe it was something else. She decided not to push it for the time being and to give him a chance to tell his story in his own time.

The wind outside grew louder. Jackson returned in a half hour. The dog started his hoarse, broken growl a few moments before the knock came at the door. Claudia had pulled her gun, but she tucked it out of sight again and let Jackson in. A blast of sandy wind came in with him, and she shut the door again quickly. The vet carried a large brown paper sack and a six-pack of Heineken. The aroma of cooked food filled the trailer.

"Cable's out already," Jackson said. "Phones too. At this point we might get cell phone reception back before anything else. I got a stash of movies in the house if you want something to watch."

"Thanks," she said. "And thanks for picking up supper."

"You're welcome. How's our boy?"

"Quiet. Eat with us?"

"Sure, why not," said Jackson.

They unlatched the dining table from the wall and lowered it. She gestured for Jackson to slide around the L-shaped couch to sit. Then she took the end, so she could get out easily if needed. The suppers were typical diner fare and substantial, two fried chicken dinners with mashed potatoes and corn, and a pot roast stew with potatoes and vegetables. Dinner rolls filled a separate bag. She popped open two bottles of beer and set one in front of Jackson, the other at her place.

"Can he have more pain medication now?" Claudia asked.

Jackson checked his wristwatch. "If you can get him to take it. Wrap it in some of the bread and dunk it in a little gravy. If he won't eat it, I can give him a shot."

She stuffed a pill in a piece of bread and sopped it with rich, dark gravy. Then she held it to the dog's nose. "Come on, Precious," she murmured. "Eat the nums-nums, or Himself has to have a nasty old shot."

The dog's bitter-chocolate eyes narrowed on her in such disgust she had to grin.

"That really how you talk to him?" Jackson bit into a chicken leg and said around a full mouth, "Can't believe the dog hasn't bitten you yet."

"I know," she said. "Can't believe it myself. Isn't he great? Think I might have to get him a rhinestone collar. He'd look good in pink." The Wyr snorted softly, but he made no move to take the morsel from her hand.

Why wouldn't he take the medicine? She tried to think of what she would do in his position. She said to him telepathically, *It's okay to take the meds. I'm Special Forces, retired, I'm armed and I'm not going to let anything happen to you. You're safe. You don't have to be in pain, and you don't need to stay alert tonight.*

Holding her gaze, he gently took the morsel from her fingers. He had to struggle to swallow it past bruised throat muscles, but he got it down.

Inexplicably his act of trust hit her hard, and her eyes grew damp. She rubbed the corner of his ear and said in a husky voice, "Thank you."

When she slid into her seat, his head was near her feet. With a near-silent grunt, he shifted so that he could rest his chin on the toe of her shoe. When she felt that slight weight come down on her foot, she held herself so stiffly, her muscles started to ache in protest.

She hated it when her eyes leaked. She would rather be shot than cry. She had been shot before, so she knew what she was talking about. And he had made her teary twice in one day.

Goddamn dog.

Chapter Three

Law

He knew he needed to make some decisions soon but he figured making one was enough for this shithole of a day. Deciding to let go, trust the woman, and take the pain medication was it. It wasn't like he could actually do much until he healed more, and the woman had saved his life. And he didn't think she was the type of grandstanding idiot to claim she'd been Special Forces if she hadn't been. She owned a gun and she knew how to use it.

Not many women became Green Berets. Of course, not many men did either. He liked what that said about her. Said she was strong, unusual.

He liked her scent too. She didn't wear any perfumes, and her clothes had been laundered with scent-free soap. He breathed in as deeply as he could. She had a clean, healthy fragrance that held a hint of gun oil.

Actually, that was kinda hot. Although "hot" was a fairly hypothetical subject at the moment. Still, serious though his wounds might be, he was only hurt; he wasn't dead.

The medication kicked in. It didn't take his pain away. It just put it at a distance and stuffed his head full of cotton so he didn't care so much. He ran down a list of his injuries. His body was one big bruise, but soft tissue healed quicker than bone, and his raw, abraded skin would be closed over by morning. The deeper damage to his throat and the other muscles from the two bullet wounds would take a bit longer.

He didn't know about the broken ribs. Without access to high-end Powerful healing, he guessed they would knit in three or four days. Since he was recovering from so many injuries at once, the breaks might take longer. More like a week, maybe ten days.

Normally a week wasn't long. Normally that amount of time might seem miraculously quick, compared to the healing time needed by the much more fragile races, such as humans or faeries.

But he didn't have a week to recover. He had about as long as it took for word to get out that he hadn't died. Not long at all.

He tried to think through his options. Exhaustion and the stuffed cotton in his head kept interfering, plus the woman and the man started talking as they ate. He focused on their conversation. He liked the woman's voice too. It was strong, clear and confident. It suited her. She seemed pure in a way that had nothing to do with all the puppies and flowers and shit that came with youthful innocence. Her purity was sharper, brighter, he thought. It had been forged in a tough fire and tempered with experience.

"Your ticket, driver's license and registration are still sitting on my kitchen counter," the male said.

"Thanks. I'll get them later."

He struggled to remember their names. Ah, that's right, the vet was Jackson. The woman had told him her name was Claudia.

Claudia. He loved that name. It suited her. There was no shortening it without turning it into something totally ridiculous and alien, yet it was feminine without being too frilly. It was strong, like the rest of her.

"That's fine," Jackson said.

What was fine? He wasn't tracking too well. Damn cotton in his head. Shouldn't have taken the meds. It messed with his thinking.

Jackson was continuing. "Was thinking about you and John when I went to pick up supper. What you said and didn't say."

"Don't know what you're talking about," said Claudia. "I didn't say anything to Rodriguez, or about him. All I said was I didn't know him, or you."

"It was more your attitude than anything else," Jackson said. "Look at us. We're perfect strangers. We still saved a dog's life, we're eating supper and drinking beer together, and you're staying in my trailer tonight."

She burst out laughing.

"All right, that sounded more suggestive than I meant it to." Jackson sounded embarrassed. "My point is, you wouldn't have done this with John. There something about how you reacted to him."

The dog made an immense effort, raised his head and took hold of the hem of her jeans with his teeth.

Claudia didn't move. "I was annoyed. I knew he was still going to ticket me even though I was just trying to save the dog's life."

He said, "Okay, that's got to be true enough. But I think it's more than that, because it wasn't just you. It was John's attitude too."

"What do you mean?"

Jackson was silent a moment. Then he said, "You know, Nirvana's like any other small town. There are a lot of personal soap operas, and half the folks who attend church go for the gossip. You know the kind of thing. Usually somebody done somebody else wrong. Or maybe they have something or someone that somebody else wants. At its heart, though, this is a simple place. This town is owned. It has one big employer, the Nirvana Silver Mining Company, and one owner of the company, Charles Bradshaw. His son, Scott Bradshaw, actually runs the mine."

"That's a lot more than I knew a couple hours ago," said Claudia. She leaned sideways to slip her hand under the table. She stroked the dog's head, her fingers moving so gently over him, he sighed and let go of his hold on her jeans. The meds made her touch seem far away, just like the pain. He wished it were otherwise. Gods, he was tired. He put his chin on her shoe again.

"As you can tell, the power structure around here is not complicated."

"Where are you going with this, Jackson?"

"I don't know." He paused. "Yes, I do. See, John has to answer to the powers that be. And Scott Bradshaw is dumb and mean. John isn't the only one affected by that, of course. Everybody in Nirvana has to bear that particular cross. Scott's father is smart and mean, which is a whole lot worse, but at least Bradshaw Senior lives in Las Vegas and pretty much stays there. Scott, though—I could see him torturing a dog. He has a hellish temper."

"Does he, now." Claudia sounded thoughtful.

"Or maybe one of his cronies would abuse an animal," Jackson said. "Scott's got four or five buddies who aren't any better than he is. So maybe one of them did this. Then John has a problem on his hands. Maybe he has to clean up other people's shit or he's the one that lands in trouble with Bradshaw Senior."

"Nobody's forcing Rodriguez to be sheriff," Claudia said. "Man's got choices."

"I know he does." Jackson sighed. "Hell, I don't even know what I'm talking about, anyway. This is just where my imagination went when I was in the diner."

"The law is a funny thing," Claudia said. "When it's fair and impartial, and it's on your side, it can be the backbone of society. But when I was in the army I saw a lot of corruption in various communities at the local level. Somebody taking the law and using it for his own ends? That never turns out well."

Shortly after that conversation, Jackson left, a gust of sand blowing in the door before he slammed it shut behind him. She cleared away the takeout containers.

The wind had picked up until it sounded an unending, mournful howl. The trailer was warm but the floor seemed chilly to her, so she collected one of the old cotton blankets she had found and shook it out over the dog's prone figure. She checked on the container that held the pot roast dinner. The meal had been too hot before, but it had since cooled to a comfortable level.

The dog had been dozing, but his eyes opened when she sat down on the floor beside him with the container and a couple of dinner rolls. Her guess had been right, the floor was chilly. She tucked a corner of the blanket over her legs. She tore off a piece of the roll, soaked it in gravy, and held it out to him. He looked at the morsel of food but didn't move.

"It must be really painful for you to swallow right now," she said. "But try a few pieces. Please. You'll get your strength back more quickly if you can eat."

He took the food with obvious reluctance. She looked away from his struggle to swallow as she prepared a second bite. She added a sliver of meat to it.

"I think we have something of a simple binary situation," she said. "Either/or, yes or no. Only this time, it's a matter of can't or won't."

She offered him the bite. He accepted it, watching her with wary, drug-glazed eyes.

"I'm not sure if you can't or won't shape-shift," she said. "My guess is you can't because you're too hurt. I could see how you might pretend to be a mundane dog, except that pretending won't get you anything. If word hasn't gotten out already that you lived, it will. Rodriguez knows that you survived the trip to the vet, and your reaction earlier told me that's not necessarily a good thing."

She offered him a piece of potato. He just looked at it. She dropped it back into the stew and held out a piece of meat. He took it carefully from her fingers and worked to swallow it.

"I'm not surprised about Rodriguez," she continued. "I could tell he was walking some kind of line earlier. He made each ethical decision as he came to it. Should he pull the gun and shoot you? How much did it matter that I was a witness? Could—or would—he really go so far as to kill me too? I don't think it was a coincidence he pulled me over just after I found you. I think he was looking for you. Maybe he's the one who tried to kill you. But that doesn't feel right." She didn't think Rodriguez would have left the dog alive beside the highway. The sheriff looked like the kind of man who also knew the impact of a well-placed bullet.

She sounded out another idea. "Maybe somebody was supposed to kill you and fucked up. Someone dumb and mean might be capable of that. Then Rodriguez was sent to make sure the job got done properly, only I found you first. That sounds plausible. But what are you doing in Nevada and why would somebody want to kill you? Logic won't tell me those things. Only you can and you won't talk. Won't, not can't, because you could tell me telepathically if you wanted to."

She held out another sliver of meat. He closed his eyes. He looked utterly exhausted, the skin around his eyes sunken. Emotion twisted in her gut. She closed the container and wiped her fingers on a napkin. "Okay," she said gently. "You get a free pass tonight. I won't push."

He was a dual-natured creature, one of the Elder Races. It was probably patronizing and even insulting to pet him as if he were a mundane dog. She struggled, but then gave in to the impulse and stroked his well-shaped head again. He responded with a deep sigh and seemed to relax a bit, as if her touch comforted him.

She supposed he could always tell her to stop. That would be one way to force him into speech. She could pet him into talking. Stroking his soft ear, she looked across the floor, at her legs crossed at the ankles, and the long length of his body.

"Precious, you are one big son of a bitch," she said with a ghost of a chuckle. "I'm sorry you don't feel like you can even tell me your name."

She was tired of hearing the sound of her own voice. It was a strain to talk so much after having been silent for days on the road. She fell quiet and listened to the wind.

That was when the strange voice came into her head.

Telepathy was a funny thing. Even though it was an entirely mental experience, the mind attributed different voices with the same kind of characteristics as it would physical ones.

The voice Claudia heard was deep and male, with a touch of an accent.

My name is Luis.

She paused in petting him, as she absorbed that. Hearing his name, even though she had already known he was Wyr, seemed to cause some kind of intangible but very important shift.

"Thank you, Luis," she said quietly. "You're going to be all right. I'll take care of you. I promise."

Luis felt a deep resonance at the words. What she said was something he might say to someone else. But there was something wrong about those words being spoken to him, something somehow backward. The cotton in his head kept him from fully connecting to why that was, and he fell asleep trying to figure it out.

Claudia felt restless and her mind kept churning over recent events. To give her hands something to do, she fetched the Tarot deck in the wooden box, along with the paperback she had bought that explained the Elder Races Tarot. She flipped through the paperback desultorily, but she had already read about the Major and Minor Arcana, and at the moment she wasn't really interested in reading the rest.

Instead, she opened the antique, painted box and pulled out the hand painted deck. As she did so, she thought back to the strange way she had acquired it.

A couple months ago in January, while she was wintering in New York, a slender woman had stopped her in the street. The city was still recovering from a major blizzard in late December. The streets were heaped with great mounds of dirty snow, and leftover Christmas and Masque decorations dotted shop windows.

She and the woman had been walking past each other, just two bundled-up pedestrians among hundreds of thousands in the frigid, snowbound city, when the woman turned suddenly and took hold of Claudia's arm.

She didn't think the other woman realized how dangerous that was. Claudia spun but managed to check her instinct for violence. She got an impression of dark, gold-tipped corkscrew curls, a warm, brown complexion in a thin, intelligent face, and hazel eyes behind wire-rim glasses that widened at her fast reaction.

"I'm sorry," the woman said. "You're probably going to think I'm crazy, but…" Claudia tensed as the woman reached in her dark leather purse, but all she pulled out was the Tarot box. She thrust it into Claudia's hands. "These want to come to you. I don't understand why. I've had them for years."

"What are you talking about?" Claudia asked. She turned the box over in her hands, opened it up and saw the deck inside.

"The cards," the woman said. She gave Claudia a smile that seemed embarrassed. "They're opinionated."

"Are you telling me these are magic?" Claudia asked. If they were, she couldn't sense it. Torn between fascination and caution, she nearly shoved the deck back into the strange woman's hands and walked away.

"Not really," said the woman. "They have a spark of Power but they're not spelled, and they're not harmful."

Claudia raised her eyebrows. "How did you know they wanted to come to me?"

"They pulled toward you. I don't know how else to describe it."

"And just what exactly do you think I'm supposed to do about it?"

"I don't know. Whatever you would normally choose to do." The woman started walking backwards, talking as she went. "I'm sorry to shove them at you and run, but I'm late to meet my fiancé. I guess if you need money, they should be worth a fair amount if you take them to the Magic District. I paid several thousand dollars for that deck over ten years ago… Oh, I really have to go— good luck to you."

Disturbed and intrigued, Claudia had gone to the Magic District to get the box and its contents appraised. Two different magic users confirmed what the woman had said, that while the antique deck had a spark of Power, it wasn't dangerous. It was also quite valuable and would be worth between eight and ten thousand dollars at auction. The third person told her the deck was dangerous and offered to take it off her hands for fifty bucks. Yeah right.

She decided to keep the deck. Despite its value, its previous owner had been willing to give it to a total stranger in order to honor the Power that was soaked into the cards. She supposed she could hang on to it for a while to see what happened. She could always sell it later.

Since then she had fallen into the habit of playing with the deck whenever she was idle. Shuffling and reshuffling the cards gave her hands something to do while she thought. Once or twice she had tried setting out one of the card spreads from the paperback, but she didn't have the learning or aptitude for reading a card spread.

She knew some general things from what the book described. The cards on the left were positive, and the cards on the right were negative. Some cards indicated the future, and some indicated the present or past. But the significance of the specific cards and their relationship to each other was beyond her, and she frankly had no interest in trying to learn more.

But then she discovered a curious thing. The seven Major Arcana, which depicted the seven Elder gods, turned up every time she laid the cards out in a basic spread: Taliesin, the god of the Dance; Azrael, the god of Death; Inanna, the goddess of Love; Nadir, the goddess of the depths or the Oracle; Will, the god of the Gift; Camael, the goddess of the Hearth; and Hyperion, the god of Law. The seven Primal Powers, the Elder Races considered them the linchpins in the universe.

They also showed up when she shuffled the deck and turned the first seven cards over. So she shuffled them again. And then again. And they still showed up.

Not once, or even most of the time.

Every. Fricking. Time.

The book didn't have a section on this occurrence. She searched online, and eventually found one posting in an obscure forum. Someone had claimed to have turned up all seven of the Major Arcana in a spread and had asked for advice. The discussion had been long, excited and involved, and filled with speculation, but in essence there was only one consensus: the spread indicated an upcoming period of time that would be filled with life-altering significance.

Like that was helpful.

Over the last couple of months, Claudia had developed an obsessive habit of shuffling and flipping over the first seven cards. The only thing that changed was the order in which the seven gods appeared.

Shuffle, flip.

She could probably develop a grift around it, make some money off some poor slob in a bar somewhere. Maybe she should consult with an experienced Tarot reader. For fifty bucks, they would probably tell her that turning up the seven Major Arcana had "life-altering significance".

Shuffle, flip.

Life altering, like maybe saving a Wyr's life. One who had been tortured and left for dead. What had been done to him really had been dumb and mean.

Shuffle, flip.

And it wasn't just one dumb, mean bastard who had done it. Claudia might not have talked much while Jackson had ministered to Luis, but she had clocked the two different-caliber bullets the vet had cut out of him, and both were from rifles. She palmed them and afterward, when she and Jackson had been washing up, she had rinsed the bullets off and slipped them into her pocket.

So there were at least two bastards involved. And like she said earlier, Luis was a big son of a bitch. One big Wyr would be more than a match for Bradshaw Junior and his dumb, mean friends, unless they shot him first.

Shuffle, flip.

So that's what they did. They shot him first and brought him down. Then they could have tapped him in the back of the head with another well-placed shot, but they hadn't.

The rest of what they did to him had been for fun.

And Rodriguez knew he was here.

She kept circling back to Rodriguez. Brutal as it sounded, the simple truth was that he would have no need to clean up a mess if it had just been a dog that had been tortured, because a mundane dog couldn't talk.

No, Rodriguez had to have gotten involved because they knew Luis was Wyr. If Luis survived, he could talk.

And for some reason, it mattered to them that he didn't.

Chapter Four

The Dance

Even as that last thought went through her mind, she was on her feet and moving out of the trailer, tucking the Glock at the small of her back. She covered her mouth and nose against the blast of sand outside as she strode across the small backyard.

Darkness had fallen and Jackson had turned on the outside lights. The illumination looked murky in the swirling sandstorm. It also looked like he had every light in his house turned on. She banged on his back door and he opened it almost immediately.

He still hadn't removed his cowboy hat. He gestured for her to step inside and shut the door as soon as she crossed the threshold. "What's up?"

She turned to face him and said, without preamble, "You need to go visit your daughter in Fresno."

"Do I?" His faded, intelligent gaze met hers. "I was getting ready to have a poker game. Got six people coming over. They'll start showing up any minute now. I expect we're gonna pull an all-nighter if you find you need anything."

She glanced around the kitchen and expelled a breath. He had brewed a fresh pot of coffee, set out snacks and cards, and pulled the chairs back around the table. Apparently Jackson had been doing more thinking as well. "Wish you'd go to Fresno instead."

"Like I said earlier, it won't be good highway driving tonight. Maybe I can leave for Fresno tomorrow, when things are looking a little clearer," said Jackson. "And when we know that dog is out of the woods."

"Maybe."

"We'll keep the noise down, but all the lights on," Jackson said. He went to the counter, scooped up her license, registration and ticket, and handed it to her. She folded it up, stuffed it in her back pocket, and stood with her hands on her hips, looking out the back window at the trailer.

Seven people. Seven witnesses, with cars lined up in the street out front and all the lights blazing in the house. Would that be enough to stave off anyone who might come by looking to silence Luis for good?

She kept coming back to Rodriguez, goddammit. If dumb and mean had realized how badly they had fucked up, they wouldn't have called Rodriguez to clean up their mess. They would have just circled back around themselves to find Luis and finish what they'd started. They must have either thought they'd already killed him or the desert would finish him off soon enough. They'd been careless.

No, Rodriguez got involved because he had a dialogue with someone else. Someone sent him out to get proof of death. And the next beast up that food chain was Bradshaw Senior.

Which meant this involved an issue that was larger than a simple hate crime or personal matter.

Was it a large enough issue that it might endanger a well-meaning veterinarian and six other innocent people? It could be. It very well could be.

Thumbs hooked in her pockets, she drummed her fingers against her hip bones. She said, "Why don't you play your poker game in the trailer? Either that, or we can move the dog into the house."

Surprise flickered over Jackson's battered features. He moved to stand behind her shoulder and looked out at the trailer too. "Why would we want to do either of those things?"

She told him, "Because I'm going out."

He frowned. "Going where?"

"Didn't you say people hang out in the bars during these storms?"

"Yeah, but maybe it's not such a good idea for you to join them tonight." He sounded troubled.

"Don't see why not." She gave him a bland smile. "I'm just going out for a beer."

The sandstorm had started to die down when she left. She took the Glock, but when she pulled into the parking lot of the first bar, after a few minutes' thought, she left the gun in her glove compartment.

Inside, she had a nonalcoholic beer, chatted with locals and learned some things.

The population number listed on Nirvana's welcome sign was misleading, since it included everyone in Nirvana County. The town itself had around five hundred residents, all of whom either worked directly for the mining company or their local businesses were indirectly dependent on it somehow.

Built on an underground spring and located near the mine, Nirvana was one of the many small towns that had been a stopping point along the Transcontinental Railroad. Now it was a stopping point for Greyhound Lines. The town boasted its own Safeway supermarket, and its two bars were located at either end of Main Street. There were also two motels, three gas stations, and a family-style diner/casino off the interstate exit.

One of the gas stations was a combination truck stop/fast-food joint/casino, open 24/7. If Claudia weren't in such a grim mood, she might have smiled. You could eat, gas up, and gamble, all at the same time. Just in case you felt you needed to do all those things in a hurry.

Another gas station sold liquor and carried a selection of movie rentals. The third hadn't yet discovered a successful enough niche to diversify from its competitors. She remembered seeing that gas station earlier. It had looked shabby and neglected.

The most important thing she learned was what Bradshaw Junior and his boys looked like. Soon as she got those descriptions, she paid for her drink and drove down Main Street to the other side of town.

It was in the second bar that she hit the jackpot.

She knew who they were as soon as she pushed through the door. Four strapping guys, each around thirty years old, stood together by the pool table. They fit perfectly the descriptions she'd been given. A couple of them held pool sticks but they weren't playing. They were drinking and talking in low voices, their expressions tense and edgy.

Shucks, looked like they weren't having a good day.

Also looked like they might be working themselves up to do something about that.

Junior was dark-haired and handsome. According to the locals, he was the spitting image of Bradshaw Senior. He stood around six-two, and he had the muscled body of a college football player, with years of self-indulgence starting to thicken him around the middle.

She paused just after stepping inside, and she stared at the foursome until one of them looked up and saw her. Just so happened, it was Junior. She liked that. She gave him a long, level look, which he returned.

Hook baited and line cast.

Then she headed for the bar. This time she ordered a real beer. The bar was much like its counterpart, casually decorated and comfortably worn. This one had black-and-white photographs of the silver mine hung on the walls. Randy Travis sang "She's My Woman" loudly over the sound system. An indefinable something separated the locals from the travelers who had stopped for the night. She wasn't sure what it was. Maybe it was how people talked to each other.

She leaned her folded arms on the bar and nursed her beer.

They kept her waiting all of ten minutes.

"Heard you found my dog," someone said behind her. "He got loose the other day, and I've been looking for him ever since. I was just fixing to go get him."

The talker was Junior, she saw as she glanced over her shoulder. He was smiling. He looked relaxed and confident, a man who was sure of his world and his place in it. He was dressed in jeans and a lined flannel shirt like the other local men, but his haircut would not have looked out of place in a country club.

One of his friends stood at his shoulder, while the other two came up on either side of her at the bar. She looked at the bartender, who had somehow become busy at the other end of the room. That was just fine with her. She wanted the bartender to stay out of the way.

She turned around to face Junior and said, "You heard wrong. He's my dog now."

Junior came closer, his big body moving with a smooth athleticism he had not yet lost. His smile deepened, his eyes full of sociopathic charm. "I don't think so," he said. "Tell me what the vet bill was, and I'll double it. In cash. Then you can hit the road again, and put this whole thing behind you."

She took a pull on her beer and set the bottle down as the guys on either side crowded closer, their expressionless faces oddly menacing. They were all taller than she was and built like football players.

She met Junior's eyes and said, "Fuck off."

Astonishment wiped the charm off Junior's face. He lunged forward until his body pressed hers back against the bar. His hands gripped the bar on either side of her, and he came nose to nose with her.

"You must be one incredibly stupid bitch," he said.

Hook swallowed.

"I know you did it," she said. Her voice was soft and even as she looked full bore and unblinking into his eyes. "You shot him, and then you beat him. Then you tied a rope around his neck and you dragged him, God knows how far. And you didn't do it alone, because there were two different-caliber rifle bullets in him, and I've got both of them. So your friends can fuck off too."

"Did you hear me offer the stupid bitch money," Junior said to the man on her left.

"Why yes, I did, Scott," said his friend. "I heard that loud and clear."

"It could have been so easy for you to walk away," Junior told her.

Tease the line out. Let the fish run.

"Yeah, I don't think so," she told him. "You can't do anything in here. It's too public. Unless you're going to fuck that up too. Really, I don't think you understand the definition of *stupid* and who it applies to."

She watched with interest as fury swallowed his handsomeness and turned him ugly. There you are, she said silently. Now you're showing your real self.

"Outside," Junior said to the others. He stepped back, and the men on either side of her suddenly moved closer, each one grabbing her by the wrist and bicep while they hid the maneuver from the rest of the bar with their bodies.

"Scream and I'll break your arm," one of them whispered.

She didn't scream.

Junior and his third friend moved in from behind. By the time they hit the door, they were almost running and had her completely lifted off the ground. She jerked, trying to get her arms free, but the pressure to her arm sockets was brutally painful.

Junior said, "Take her out back."

She looked up as they rushed her around the corner of the bar. The storm had died down, but the night sky was still sullen and overcast. A couple of cars were parked out back near a spiky tangle of desert shrubbery and a line of yucca trees.

The spot was a little too close to public activity for her taste, but it was still private. None of the other buildings or houses was nearby, and with the loud bar music, no one inside would hear any screams. The one weakness would be if someone arrived in the parking lot around front and heard something, but there were a lot of ways to muffle noise.

"What I want to know is why you did it," she said.

"Who the fuck cares what you want to know?" Junior said contemptuously.

"There's a story to this," she said. "And it wasn't personal. Rodriguez wouldn't have gotten involved if it had been, not unless you pulled something royally asinine, like getting caught with your dick out in public.

Not that you're beyond that, at least from everything I've heard."

"I'm going to enjoy making you hurt," he said. "And I'm going to hurt you a lot."

"No, Rodriguez would have gotten involved only if his job depended on it," she continued. "That would mean this matters to your father somehow, and I think what matters to your father is the silver mine. How'm I doing so far? Am I hot or am I cold?"

"You're dead fucking meat, is what you are." He said to the others, "Right here."

She tightened her abdomen muscles against a blow. They slammed her down, stomach first, against the trunk of one car and held her bent over. The cold of the metal trunk bit through her jeans and sweatshirt. Junior moved up behind her, putting his hands at her waist.

Time to reel in the fish.

She started to laugh. "Wow, are you inept. You can't even do this by yourself."

He grabbed her by the hair, cruelly pulling at the roots. "Back up," he snapped at the two that held her arms. They let go of her as he pinned her with the weight of his body. He hissed in her ear, "You should have stayed silent. Should have moved on. Should have taken the money when I offered it. There are so many 'should haves' you should have done, so I figure that means you asked for this. You'll be begging before we're finished with you."

As he talked he reached around her waist to the front of her jeans, searching with hard fingers for the fastening.

She didn't have enough room to leverage out a serious blow. No normal human woman could have broken his hold.

But she wasn't quite a normal human woman.

Telekinesis can be a finicky Power. Some people could manipulate things from a distance away. Others, usually those with a lesser degree of Power like her, needed to be able to touch what they wanted to shift.

Since Claudia's aptitude for telekinesis wasn't much, she'd had to work to figure out what she could and couldn't do. Someone else might not have bothered, but the army was interested in her talents, and they spent a lot on training her. She was interested too, and she worked hard at every opportunity they gave her. As a result, what she could do was well thought out and well practiced.

She could hit like a motherfucker. Kick like one too. From a standstill, she could throw a roundhouse punch that could bring a two-ton troll to its knees.

She had to be careful when she was fighting those of the Elder Races who were faster than she was, and whose bodies were more durable. She had to think strategically. Turned out, she was good at doing that too. Fighting was a dance like no other, as each one of her opponents became her partner for a deadly brief period of time.

She had maybe eight inches of space to work with. That was more than enough. She struck back with her elbow and hit Junior's midsection.

Junior coughed out all his breath and crumpled to the ground. She twisted around.

He had no air in his lungs with which to speak. His bulging gaze was astonished. It asked her, *What the fuck?*

So she answered his question. She showed him what the fuck. She kicked him in the chest, using her foot to leverage his body weight. The blow lifted him off the ground and slammed him into the back of the building several yards away. When his three friends rushed her, she showed them what the fuck too.

When she finished with the would-be rapists and walked away, all four of them were on the ground. Two of them were unconscious, and one of them was crying.

Because Junior wasn't the only one who had a hellish temper.

Claudia had a hellish temper too.

Chapter Five

Sacrifice

"Wake up, Precious," a male said.

Luis came awake instantly. Once again, he almost lunged to attack but he managed to check himself before he tore off the other male's face. It was the older man, the veterinarian. Jackson. She wouldn't like it if Luis hurt him.

Jackson was a smart man. He had jerked back as Luis came awake. "Here now, none of that," he said gruffly. Despite his obvious age and experience, the human didn't sound nearly as confident as Claudia had when she'd shushed Luis. "I've got something for you."

Luis was in the trailer, but Claudia wasn't. A strange male, also human but much younger than Jackson, stood well away from them both, his nervous scent spiking the air.

Luis bared his teeth. He was groggy, confused and angry that the men had gotten into the trailer and Claudia had slipped away without waking him up. That would never have happened if he hadn't been injured and heavily medicated. She had promised to protect him. Where had she gone?

Then Jackson showed him three liquid-filled vials. He stared. Jackson offered him the chance to sniff them but he didn't bother. In his mind's eye, the vials shone with Power.

"Don't worry, son," Jackson said. "I'm not gonna talk baby talk at you and ask if you'll take the num-nums. I have a feeling you'd bite me a whole lot sooner'n you'd bite her. Feel like having a drink?"

"That's all we had at the Urgent Care Clinic, Dan," said the strange man. "You didn't tell me why you needed it. You're not really going to give thousands of dollars worth of healing potion to a dog, are you?"

"Yeah, Stewart, I think I am," said Jackson. With a near-silent grunt, he levered himself down on one knee in front of Luis. "At least I'm gonna give him one to start with. We'll see how that goes."

"It's going to take at least twenty-four hours for the clinic to replace those," said Stewart. "Who's gonna pay for them?"

"Not real sure about that part," Jackson said. "I feel certain the money will come from somewhere. If nothing else, I'm betting his new owner will chip in. Worse comes to worse, I'll pay for them myself. But I don't think I'll have to."

"He's a dog."

"That's the thing. I don't think he's just any dog, Stew."

Luis watched intently as Jackson uncapped a potion and poured it into a shallow dish. He pushed upright enough so that he could drink, ignoring the harsh explosion of pain that his movement caused. He had his nose in the dish almost before Jackson could set it on the floor. Breathing shallowly, he lapped at the small, valuable amount of liquid and forced his swollen throat muscles to work. Power exploded like a sunburst inside him, flaring outward until his raw, abraded skin felt like it was on fire.

"Want another one?" Jackson asked.

Luis nodded.

"Well, fuck me dead and gone," Stewart said. The other human sounded shaken.

"A heartfelt, if unsavory, sentiment," Jackson said. He blew out a breath and poured a second one in the dish, and then the third.

Luis gulped them down.

"Mind if I take some of these bandages off?"

Luis growled, still drinking.

"Oh-kay," Jackson said, drawing back. "Guess you'll handle taking the bandages off yourself."

Luis finished the last of the potion and lay back down, panting as the healing spell spread through his abused body. Broken ribs knitted, and torn muscle and skin mended. Healing potions did an amazing amount of good, but they weren't pain-free. He felt like his whole body was immersed in flames.

Luckily the humans knew enough to stand well back and let the process occur, because for a short time he felt blinded, out of control. If either had been foolish enough to touch him, he really might have savaged them.

A formless amount of time later, the flames in his body eased. He stretched carefully, taking note of the changes. The pain in his rib cage and throughout his body was now a dull ache. He wasn't completely healed. His injuries had been too severe, and the Power in stored healing potions was not as potent as fresh spells thrown by a healer.

But the disorientation from his injuries and the medication had burned away, and his mind could finally function again. He could take a deep breath without a stabbing pain in his chest, his raw abrasions had closed over, and the bullet wounds had closed enough so that they were no longer bleeding.

All of that might mean the difference between life and death, because now he was no longer helpless.

He nosed under the blanket to tear at the bandages with his teeth. Then he rolled over, onto all four paws, and shape-shifted. He stood as he changed, instinctively ducking his head in case the ceiling of the trailer was too low for his height.

Both Jackson and Stewart took a couple steps back, staring. Yeah, he got that kind of reaction from some people, more often from other males. He stood at six and a half feet tall when he wasn't slouching, and his body was all muscle.

Usually females took a few steps closer.

Stewart whispered, "Holy snot."

"Where did she go?" Luis asked Jackson. He rotated his shoulders carefully and stretched stiff neck muscles.

"She went to the bars," Jackson said. "Been gone about an hour now."

Luis snapped out a curse while he ran another mental check on his condition. He needed to get to his supplies, but first he needed to get to Claudia to make sure she was all right.

What the hell was she thinking, going out? She had seen up close and personal what Scott Bradshaw and his friends were capable of doing, and thanks to Rodriguez, her role in today's events would be well-known by now.

The nearest bar was almost a mile away. Could he run it? Yeah, he could, but it would be uncomfortable, since his ribs were still healing. In another day, maybe two, that wouldn't matter and he would be able to run the day away, but he wasn't there quite yet.

"I need clothes," he said. "And I need to borrow your car."

Jackson shook his head. "Sorry to disappoint you, son, but I ain't got any clothes that'll fit you."

"He might be able to squeeze into some sweatpants," Stewart said. "Or a loose pair of boxers, if you wear them. You know, to at least cover the basics…" The human waved a hand vaguely in the direction below Luis's waist, looking away.

Another time the human's discomfort with his nudity might have made Luis grin, but not now. His muscles were jumping with adrenaline, and every word they spoke felt like a delay. He could change back to a dog and make that uncomfortable run for the bars, but he didn't want to give anybody plausible deniability for shooting a dangerous stray they found running loose through town. Better to stay in human form and take a vehicle.

From outside the trailer, another man called, "Dan, Stewart—what's keeping you back there? Are we playing poker any time soon?"

"I'll try on anything you've got," Luis said to Jackson.

"Right," Jackson said.

Even as the two humans turned to leave, lights flashed across the trailer windows. A car pulled around the corner of the house and rolled to a stop. The headlights cut out. Luis gently nudged the curtain away from the window, looking outside as the trickle of adrenaline running through his veins became a flood.

The car was a 1984 BMW. Claudia climbed out of the driver's seat. She still wore jeans and a black sweatshirt, her lean, graceful body and hard, composed face illuminated by the light that shone from the house's windows. Metal glinted briefly as she tucked her Glock at the small of her back. Luis relaxed as his immediate sense of urgency eased. He let the curtain fall back into place.

"Be right back," Jackson said. Stewart had already stepped out, the frigid night air swirling into the trailer's interior.

Luis nodded. He glanced at the older male as he said, "Thanks. For everything."

Jackson returned the nod then shut the door behind him as he left.

Luis twitched the curtain aside again. He watched Jackson intercept Claudia, and they stood close together, talking. Claudia glanced at the trailer.

He turned away and looked around the interior. After a moment's hesitation, he strode over to the shadowed alcove of the bed, took a sheet, folded it a couple of times then wound it around his waist. You know, to at least cover the basics.

As he knotted it, the trailer door opened again and Claudia stepped inside, talking as she entered. "Jackson told me about the healing potions and that you were able to—" Her voice cut off abruptly.

He turned to face her, one eyebrow raised, and a vain part of him felt intensely satisfied as she looked as poleaxed as Jackson and Stewart had, her vivid green gaze stricken.

Then one corner of her beautiful mouth lifted. She said, "Boy howdy, Precious, you really are one big son of a bitch."

"Yes," he said.

He walked over to her, moving gently. The distance was not far, perhaps four paces. Her expression changed and grew wary, eyes watchful, but, he was glad to see, she didn't retreat like Jackson and Stewart had. Ready to pull back at any sign of aversion, he bent and tilted his head. He noticed she held her breath, but he didn't. He inhaled deeply her warm scent that carried a hint of gun oil and now held a hint of beer.

So goddamn hot. And that was no longer hypothetical.

He pressed his lips lightly, quickly, to the high, firm curve of her cheekbone and drew back to look into her eyes. He said quietly, "Thank you for saving my life."

The stiff wariness eased from her long body. She gave him a faint but real smile. There were tiny laugh lines in her smooth, tanned skin, at the corners of her mouth and her eyes.

"You're welcome, Luis."

Really shaken for the first time that evening, Claudia tried to hide the impact that Luis in his human form had on her.

He was so tall, she noticed he had to be careful that he didn't scrape his head on the trailer's ceiling. His body was massive, heavy muscles overlaid on strong, sturdy bones, with a wide, powerful chest that tapered to a long, washboard stomach. His smooth, brown, silken-looking skin wrapped the whole package like the world's most extravagant Christmas gift, and that sheet he'd knotted at his lean hips was the bow. He had dark, bitter-chocolate eyes, boldly molded features and a mouth that was so full and sensual, it should have looked girlish but didn't. His thick, black, gleaming hair held a hint of curl. It was a touch too long for the style he wore and flopped in his eyes, as though he were a couple weeks' late in getting it cut.

As he walked toward her, he moved with a fighter's easy, athletic confidence, and when he brushed her cheek, his mouth was very warm against her chilled skin.

She was used to big, tough men, and experienced with commanding them in combat missions. In some ways, Luis's physical presence was so damn familiar it was comforting on a visceral level. That was disturbing all on its own, because her gut insisted that she recognized him and his presence filled a hole that had been inside of her ever since she had lost the others in her unit and retired.

As if that weren't enough to knock her off balance, his presence had an intense vitality filled with a sexuality that ran dark and hot. It was sultry, powerful. It was knowledgeable. He carried that knowledge in his DNA, and it manifested in every languid, graceful move of his body and in those dark, intelligent eyes.

This was a man who'd had a whole lot of sex and he really, really liked it. And why wouldn't he? By the time he hit puberty, every female he met and probably several of the males would have fallen over in invitation the moment they laid eyes on him.

And she was not immune either to his particularly potent brand of alchemy.

She had not felt sexual interest or desire in over three years. She had really been okay with the thought that perhaps that part of her life was over, which made it doubly shocking to have her sexuality come roaring back to life like a lit match thrown on a lake of kerosene. Heat washed through her body, and she could tell by his small smile that he knew it. He would be able to tell by her scent she was attracted to him.

The final sucker punch? He was so goddamn young.

Goddamn. *Young.*

Good Christ, even taking into account that he was Wyr and not human, she was fairly confident that he was somewhere in his mid-twenties.

Which meant she was a good fifteen years older than he was.

Fifteen years. It was actually, physically possible that she might be old enough to be his mother.

She turned away. She didn't know what to do with her hands. She looked down at them. They were shaking. She clenched them into fists and willed the shaking to stop.

"Jackson said you went out to the bars," he said. With that slight touch of accent, his voice was just like the rest of him, low and dark and sinful like melted chocolate.

What happened to that insulation she had worked so hard to maintain for the last few years? It had been stripped away by the desert sun and an animal's suffering, and now she felt raw and critically vulnerable. She had to clench her teeth a moment before she could reply.

"I bought you—us—some time," she said.

"How?" He was light on his feet and so silent she didn't even know that he had moved until she heard the fridge door open. "Mind if I have some of this tea?"

"Help yourself." Having gotten herself marginally under more control, she turned around. His immense back was still marred with faint marks where the skin was newly healed, and a shadow of muscle rippled as he twisted the cap off the bottle of tea and tilted his head back to drink. His skin would be warm. She wondered if it was as silken as it looked, and she closed her eyes against the sight. She remembered he had asked her a question, and she told him, "I attracted the attention of Bradshaw Junior and company."

In the next instant, she felt his hands close over her shoulders. God, he was so fast. His grip was very large and strong. If anyone else had grabbed her like that, she would have put them on the floor, but she didn't do that this time. Instead, she just opened her eyes.

He looked tense, dark gaze concerned. "What did they do?"

"They were working themselves up to come after you," she said. "I was worried they might try something like that. The sandstorm had blown in, the phone lines were down, and you were too bad off to travel. I had no idea Jackson would become so innovative, and scare up some healing potion. So I got them alone, and I broke some bones."

"Broke some bones," he said. His face went blank.

She smiled. "Someone should find them before morning. If they aren't headed to the nearest ER by now, they will be soon. Luis, they are out of commission. That will draw attention from Bradshaw Senior, which will probably make things worse in the long run, but with cell reception and landlines down, someone will have to drive the news out. I also expect that Rodriguez will show up here sooner or later, but I figured it was the right price to pay, so that you, Jackson and his poker buddies would be safe for the night. I wouldn't want to relax too much in case Rodriguez gets extra enthusiastic, but I think things should be quiet enough until dawn."

"You're sure," he said. His grip had become bruising. She didn't think he realized it. "You're sure they're out of commission."

She found her footing again. Suddenly calm and steady, she held his gaze. She said gently, "I'm quite sure. I knew what I was doing, and I promise you, I put them down hard."

The expression on his face had turned raw, and those beautiful dark eyes of his filled with a remembered nightmare. He whispered, "Damn, I wish I could have seen that."

His pain reached her again. She had to swallow because a lump had grown in her throat. If she could just get some time alone, she might be able to find a way to insulate herself from shit like this.

He still gripped her shoulders hard. She put her hands over his, her palms sliding over their wide, corded strength. "I wish you could have seen it too," she said. "Right now, though, you need to explain to me what's going on. It has something to do with the mine, doesn't it?"

That snapped his gaze back to the present.

He said, "Yes."

A quick rap sounded at the door, then it opened and Jackson stepped in, carrying a bundle of clothes. "I dunno, Precious," Jackson said. "I guess you might be able to find something in this to tide you over for the night. Do you still need the keys to my truck?"

A sudden twinkle lit Claudia's green gaze, and Luis bit back a grin. Reluctant to break the connection with her, he didn't look away, nor did he release his hold. He said, "My name is Luis Alvaraz. Now that Claudia is back safe, apparently the transportation issue is no longer quite so urgent."

"Huh," said Jackson. "Well, that's got to be a good thing, right?"

"Yes, it is," Luis said. "For the moment."

Then he had to give in to the inevitable as Claudia pulled gently out of his hold. She said to Jackson, "I still want you to leave for Fresno, as quickly as possible. Would you do that, please?"

Jackson nodded thoughtfully. "Guess we no longer need that all-night poker game, do we?"

"No," Luis said. He accepted the bundle of clothes from the older male and looked through them. He added, "Please tell Stewart that I will make sure his clinic is reimbursed for the healing potions."

"Will do," Jackson said, and he paused. "You ever gonna tell me what's going on?"

"There's trouble with the mine," Luis said. He glanced at Claudia and fell silent.

Jackson poked his tongue in his cheek, and looked back and forth between the two of them. Then he sighed. "All right, I'll leave, but only if you promise to tell me the whole story sometime."

"I promise." Luis offered his hand and said gravely, "I owe you more than I can repay."

Jackson shook his hand. "So that means I can sock you with your own vet bill?"

He grinned. "I expect you to."

Then Jackson and Claudia looked at each other. Jackson's voice turned gruff. "You're not gonna just disappear when my back is turned, are you?"

She shook her head, her eyes smiling. "I owe you too, at least a few Heinekens. Maybe even a diner dinner."

"Right," Jackson said. He heaved a sigh as he looked around the trailer. "Don't bother to lock up when you leave. I keep hoping somebody'll steal that old TV."

Chapter Six

Death

Claudia followed Jackson to the door. Luis turned away, giving the other two their moment alone. He shook out a pair of faded blue sweatpants, held them against his waist and considered the length. They ended mid-calf.

The door opened and closed. Then Claudia expelled a soft gust of air, and he knew without looking that she was laughing. "You're going to look like the Incredible Hulk."

"I know," he said.

"Give me those," she said. "I'll hack off the elasticated hem."

He handed them over and inspected the T-shirts in the bundle. They were all too small for the width of his shoulders. He gave up on the clothes, tossed them aside, and went to raid the fridge for the beef dinner. Suddenly he was ravenous. He didn't bother to heat the meal in the microwave. He found a fork and started shoveling food in his mouth.

Claudia remained silent. Without looking at her directly, he was aware of everything she did, every breath she took. She picked up the blankets from the floor, folded them and set them in the shadowed alcove on the bed. Then she rolled up her sleeping bag. She didn't waste anything, not a single motion in anything she did or a single word urging him to explain. She waited for him to speak in his own time and every spare, fluid movement she made was pure poetry.

Fuck, his whole body tightened at the sight. He wanted her more badly than he had wanted anyone or anything before in his life, and to be frank, up until this point, he had been a promiscuous bastard. Desire was a fire dancing underneath his skin.

All too soon the dinner was gone. He used the last of the rolls to sop up the cold gravy and gazed at the empty container. Then Claudia spoke, sounding amused, "There's more food in the fridge. Eat anything you want. Eat everything."

He gave her a grateful look and dove into the fridge to polish off all the lunch meat, a half loaf of bread and several individual containers of yogurt. He ate quickly, to fuel his taxed body rather than for enjoyment. He was just finishing the last container of yogurt when he heard an odd noise, and he remembered he had heard it earlier as well.

Shuffle, flip.

He looked at Claudia, sitting at the table on the end of the L-shaped couch. She had finished hacking off the elasticated hems of the sweatpants and set the pants on the table. Now she was shuffling a deck of cards. She flipped over the first seven cards, scooped them up, reshuffled the deck and flipped over the top seven cards again. The deck gave off a faint glow of Power.

Intrigued, he walked over to her, and his reaction to her proximity was so strong, his cock stiffened and began to tent the sheet. Quickly he snatched up the sweatpants and held them in a casual way so that they draped in front of his groin.

Claudia looked up. He noted with deep satisfaction that she glanced at his bare chest and averted her gaze quickly. She had so much innate poise that any slight, telltale sign of reaction she had was as loud to him as a shout, and her clean scent, still with that hint of gun oil, now carried dusky notes of sexual attraction.

He loved it. He loved her. The carved, sensual maturity of her features was totally unlike the girlish, rounded faces of the young women he had known. She was so far beyond anyone he had ever been involved with, complex and nuanced, sleek as a bullet and just as dangerous. He'd had no idea that someone could embody everything he admired and also capture every ounce of his desire, until she had.

He knew without being conceited that nature had been prodigious in its gifts to him. He had more than his fair share of looks, physical and intellectual strengths, and abilities. Until now he had cruised through life at half-throttle. He played at dating and wallowed in sex, and it all came too easily for him.

It was all too simple, until he encountered Claudia. Now something that had been curled tight inside of him and asleep his whole life awoke, and expanded, and said, *Now* there's *a challenge worth striving for*.

And hell's bells, his body was out of control. He could not get his flag to fly at anything below half-mast.

He felt the sudden urge to growl, bend over and kiss her lavishly. He wanted to fling all the rest of the world's considerations away. He wondered what she would do if he did, if she would kiss him back or push him away... Man, he had to grab at the nonsense galloping around in his head and rein it in hard.

Because the rest of the world's considerations mattered, so much so he had shed blood and nearly lost his life over them.

Her attention had turned back to what she was doing. He watched her deal out the first seven cards from the top of the deck, and he recognized the god on each card as she turned it over. Nadir, Camael, Hyperion, Taliesin, Will, Azrael, and Inanna. The Depths, the Hearth, Law, the Dance, the Sacrifice, Death, and Love.

Then she scooped them up, shuffled the deck— really shuffled it, he saw—and flipped over the first seven cards, and all the gods appeared again.

Well, damn.

"What are you doing?" he asked, growing fascinated, despite his runaway hormones.

She said, "I'm giving my hands something to do until you're ready to talk." Was her voice a touch huskier as she replied?

He could give her hands something to do. It almost fell out of his mouth. Somebody should hit him.

He gestured to the cards laid out on the table. "How are you doing that?"

She shook her head. "I don't know. The cards have been doing that ever since someone in New York gave them to me."

He held his palm a few inches over hers as she handled the cards. Warm, aged Power pressed gently against his palm. "These are old," he said. "Really old. How long have you had them?"

"Since January. Some strange woman stopped me in the street, told me the cards wanted to come to me and pushed the box into my hands."

"Objects of Power often have wills of their own, and they influence the world in ways we don't understand," he said. She frowned, clearly not liking that thought. He asked, "What happened to the woman who gave them to you?"

She shrugged. "I don't know. That was the last I saw of her, and the cards have been doing this ever since. I found a discussion about it in an online forum. The general opinion was that it meant upcoming events would have 'life-altering significance'. I feel like the cards are shouting at me, only I have no idea what they're saying."

Life-altering significance. Yeah, he could agree with that, but for all seven of the Major Arcana to keep showing up repeatedly, he was pretty sure the significance was about much more than one person.

Somehow she had ended up in Nirvana at exactly the right time to save his life. As an old object of Power, the deck might be exerting influence on the world in ways that had nothing to do with her understanding what the cards might be trying to tell her. He had heard sacred stories of items that the gods threw into the world to enact their will. The Machinae, they were called. The machines.

But those were legends. As far as he could tell, this was just a deck of cards.

"When we have time, I'll do a real reading for you," he told her.

Her head snapped up. "You know how to read the Tarot?"

"I'm not as good as my grandmother. She's a *bruja*," he said. At her blank expression, he added, "A witch. She lives in New Mexico. I learned what I know from her, since she raised me." Talk about nature's prodigious gifts. He hadn't even grown up poor. A competent bruja made good money, and his grandmother lived in a stylish three-bedroom ranch in a suburb of Albuquerque. She'd paid all of his college tuition and even indulged his serious obsession with snowboarding.

Claudia set aside the cards, ran her fingers through her sleek, pale hair and massaged the back of her head in a tired-looking gesture. "So what are you doing getting shot and beat up in Nevada, Precious?"

Arousal pulsed again as he watched her, and his unruly penis stiffened further. He wanted to push her hands away and take over the massage, to soothe away that tiredness until she turned to him with as much desire as he felt. He wanted any damn excuse to put his hands on her again. Fuck. He pivoted and stalked down the miniscule hall toward the bed alcove until he was out of her sight.

"I'm a Peacekeeper with the Elder tribunal," he said. He snapped the sheet from around his waist, wadded it and threw it hard at the bed.

"You're with the Elder tribunal police force? That's an elite posting."

For crying out loud, his cock jumped just at the sound of her voice. "I'm not a senior officer. This was supposed to be a minor assignment."

"Involving the mine."

He palmed his erection, thought of her sitting just a few steps away, and his hand might have slipped a little so that he stroked himself once or three times.

Yeah, he was pretty sure that masturbating as he talked with her while she was unaware of it was sixteen ways to wrong. Which also had abso-fucking-lutely nothing to do with the greater issues at hand. As it were. He turned and let his body fall forward until his forehead hit the wall with an audible *thunk*.

Claudia said, "You all right?"

"Yeah," he said hoarsely. "I need to splash off some of this antiseptic smell. I'll be just a sec."

He sidled into the Lilliputian-sized bathroom, flipped on the cold water and stepped into the shower. The shock of frigid spray was like a slap in the gut, and just what he needed. After ninety seconds and a swipe or two with the soap, he stepped out, toweled off and yanked on the sweatpants. They were tight all over, stretching across his thighs and buttocks, and they were extremely snug across his pelvis, but at least they provided a minimal kind of covering.

This time when he strode back into the living area, Claudia's gaze fell lower than his bare chest. For the briefest moment she looked stricken again. He could have sworn a touch of color washed over her cheeks.

Do *not*, he said sternly to his cock.

For a wonder, this time his cock listened to him.

She bent her head and rubbed the back of her neck. Then she looked at him from underneath her brows, and her gaze was steady and level. Damn, this woman had emotional ballast. Was he going to find everything about her a crazy kind of hot?

"Luis, we need to talk about the invisible elephant in the trailer, because there isn't room for it here," she said.

That sounded like it might be a prologue to a brush-off. He wasn't sure, since he hadn't ever been on the receiving end of a brush-off before. He decided he wasn't going to be on the receiving end of one this time either, and he went on the offensive.

"I know," he said. "I'm insanely attracted to you, but we don't have time and it isn't appropriate right now."

He had surprised her. Her sleek eyebrows rose. "No, it isn't."

"Since we have more important things to think about, we should shelve this as a topic of conversation." Unable to resist touching her again, he laid a hand on her shoulder. She turned her head and looked at his hand, then up at him. As her gaze came up, his head swooped down, and he kissed that clever, strong woman. As he did so, he poured every ounce of his hunger into it. His mouth did a quick recon as he learned the touch and shape of her lips. He could feel the shock of his touch jolt through her body. Her lips moved under his, either to cuss him out or kiss him back, and walking that line was so damned hot. He pulled back a fraction, breathing hard, and said huskily, "So we'll talk about this later."

Dusky color darkened her fine-grained skin. "Luis," she said, very low, in a warning he would be all too pleased to ignore, and wouldn't it be a fine thing if she turned out to be more than he could handle, if she could make him stretch and reach farther than he had ever reached before.

"Now to get back to the subject at hand," he said.

There was that hand again. Seriously, someone should hit him hard.

But even though all of his instincts were driving him forward, he forced himself to straighten and pull back.

Because he didn't actually believe they had until dawn.

If someone had asked her at breakfast what her day was going to be like, her answer would have been far different from how it had turned out so far. She contemplated Luis thoughtfully while her lips burned from that smoldering kiss. He had pulled away before she could overcome the shock of it, and the shock wasn't just that he had kissed her. Her own forceful reaction sent her reeling inwardly.

What to do. She could pack up her car and leave. She didn't have to have answers. Her unit hardly ever got a big-picture explanation when they were sent on assignment. Information had always been on a need-to-know basis.

Car doors slammed outside, and the house lights darkened. One final engine started, a vehicle pulled out of the driveway, and Jackson was well on his way.

She could leave now. Jackson would be fine after a visit in Fresno, and Luis was remarkably better. He was actually on his feet again.

On his bare feet. The material from the aged sweatpants strained over every single muscle and bulge from his waist downward, and the thick biceps in his arms bunched as he crossed his arms over a wide, bare chest. He had retreated until he leaned back against the counter, watching her intently.

"Tell me why I shouldn't leave now," she said.

He said immediately, "Because I need you."

Hell, she knew that. He had no weapon, and she wasn't giving him hers. Damn it, the man wasn't even decently dressed and it had to be thirty degrees outside. But it wasn't what he said. It was how he said it, while he watched her like a hungry wolf.

"Fine," she snapped. "But if you don't tell me what's going on with that mine in the next five minutes, I'll shoot you myself."

A white grin slashed across his handsome face. It disappeared almost at once.

"The Nirvana Silver Mining Company has been in operation for almost a hundred and sixty years," he said. "It's been owned by the Bradshaw family that entire time. I won't bore you with how complicated and time-consuming it can be to obtain and maintain mining permits. What's relevant is, an area has got to be surveyed before a mine can go into production. It's important to establish legal boundaries of ownership, especially when you're talking about gems and precious metals. Those boundaries never include Other lands, so crossover passages have to be mapped and the entrances clearly defined."

She frowned. "Okay. All of that makes sense. I know federal law states that Other lands can't be owned by inhabitants on this side. That property belongs to whoever—or whatever—may reside on the other side."

"Yes," said Luis. "And if the Other land is uninhabited, then the land belongs to nobody."

"I'm with you so far," she said.

"The Office of the Elder tribunal holds records of every known crossover passage in the US. It also holds the original surveyor maps for active and inactive mines. There's no crossover passageway on any of the original surveyor maps for the Nirvana Silver Mining Company," he said. "But they have one now."

She sat back in her seat. "How did that happen? Was the original surveyor bribed?"

"I don't know," he said.

"And you were supposed to come to investigate that? That's no minor assignment."

He shook his head. "No, sensing the crossover passage was a surprise. I was actually supposed to conduct a cursory inspection of the mining operation, since nobody expected me to find anything. The mine inspection is part of a larger investigation. There's been an influx of magic-sensitive silver on the black market in the US, and reports of an increase overseas as well. The tribunal is working as part of an international effort to track down the source."

Silver had an affinity for holding magic spells and it could be used as a repository for Power. Silver from an Other land was especially magic-sensitive and highly prized. Magic-sensitive silver was more valuable than gold. "And you weren't expecting to find anything because of the original surveyor reports," she said.

"Exactly," he said. He looked wry as he ran his fingers through his hair. "I was going to tour the company's office, have a quick look through their financials for the last couple of years, eat some steaks and expense it, and watch some HBO."

She watched the thick, dark wavy hair fall back into his eyes and felt a pulse of arousal. Disconcerted, she shifted in her seat. "What happened?"

"Scott Bradshaw," he said. His sensual mouth twisted. "The company property is fenced off, of course. The manager's office is located right by the entrance, far enough away from the mine operation that I didn't sense any crossover magic from there. But Bradshaw stalled. First, he wouldn't let me on the property, and then he balked at letting me see the financials. He acted just squirrelly enough that after my official inspection, I decided to camp a night or two and keep an eye on the property."

Luis was not just sex on a Popsicle stick. He was smart, and that was what she found so damn sexy. Not that she went for younger men, or was even interested in sex. She rubbed her face. No, this was not what she had expected out of her day. "What did you see?"

Luis checked out the contents of the fridge again and pulled out the last two bottles of tea. He handed her one. "I saw food trucks entering the property at night," he said. "Frito-Lay. Dolly Madison. ConAgra."

She considered that. "Does the company run the mine twenty-four seven?"

He opened his tea and drank. "No."

She tapped a finger on the table. "Then they aren't running a cafeteria where they need all that food. Could they be using the trucks for smuggling?"

"That thought occurred to me," Luis said. "Then I had another thought." His expression had turned grim. "What if they did need all that food? If they did, who would they be feeding, and where are they? Yesterday I kept a head count of the miners who came to work in the morning, and the same number of people left again at the end of the day."

She narrowed her eyes on him. "Do you think there are people on the other side?"

He met her gaze. "Claudia, I don't think there are any good answers to the food truck question."

"Jesus," she muttered. Her mind raced. Food trucks could be a cover-up for anything, weapons or drugs, magic-sensitive silver or people. What was happening on the other side of that passageway? Were there undocumented workers? Captive workers? *Slaves?*

"You know, I liked philosophy when I was in college," he said quietly. "But I once read a phrase in a class that I never understood. The article talked about natural disasters. You know, floods, earthquakes, that sort of thing, and called them 'natural evil'. But just because those things might devastate us, that doesn't make them evil."

"You mean because they're occurrences?" she asked.

"Exactly," Luis said. "They just happen. I think natural evil is our capacity for meanness, when we make the choice to do things that cause great harm. Like the Scott Bradshaws of the world." He gave her a small, twisted smile. "There's not much more to tell before I got shot. I scaled the fence and got close enough to the actual mine that I felt the crossover passage. I scouted around but couldn't find it. I had just changed and was running back to the fence when they tagged me. I fucked up somehow. One of them saw me change, or they sensed I was Wyr. An animal of my breed shouldn't have been inside the fence. Something."

The memory of the nightmare was back in his face. She clenched her hands, resisting the urge to go over to him and offer comfort. Then somehow she wasn't resisting any longer, and she was on her feet, walking over to him. She put her hand on his warm, bare arm.

This time he covered her hand with his, pressing lightly on her fingers.

"I need you to drive me as close as you can to my campsite," he said. He looked into her eyes. His own gaze was clear and steady. "I have supplies, clothes and weapons. I can jog the rest of the distance. My Jeep is there, off-road. Then I need for you to drive out of the area too. Will you do that, please?"

She said, comfortably, "Fuck, no."

He was pissed. He was royally pissed. She could see it in the angle of his shoulders and the way he held his jaw. Well, he was just going to have to deal with it.

She tried her sat phone without much hope. She wasn't surprised to find she still didn't have a signal.

One or two stars had begun to show although the sky was still mostly overcast, turning the landscape into dull shadows. In the early hours of the morning, any residual heat from the day was long gone. She found the cold air bitter. When they climbed in the car, she put the heater on high. Soon after, he turned it down and began to argue with her.

She maintained her silence, made the turns when he told her to and kept watch for unwanted company. Finally she told him, mildly enough, "I'm going to smack you upside the head if you don't stop."

When she glanced at him, his eyes glittered and his shadowed face was hard, and that expression was even sexier than his flirting.

He took a strand of her hair and tucked it behind her ear. "I'm not going to stop."

She refused to hear nuances in that. She said, "You need to quit reacting with your emotions and think of what is optimal."

"Optimal," he spat.

She reached up to pull his hand away from her hair. "The optimal thing would be for you to drive out and take my sat phone with you. You keep trying the phone until you get a signal. You're the one with the official status, the contacts and the authority. You'll get help here on the ground much quicker than I would."

Somehow she hadn't let go of his hand. His long warm hands curled around hers, and she drove one-handed. "And you?" His tone was still short, and he didn't like what she was saying, but at least he was listening.

"Worst case scenario," she said, "we can hope it's not true, but we have to act as if it is. What if there are people across that passageway in the Other land? The company will have a store of commercial mining explosives on site. What would you do if you thought you were in danger of getting caught, and you wanted to cover your tracks?"

His grip tightened until she was in danger of losing feeling in her fingers. She could hear his breathing. "What is your solution?" he asked at last.

She squeezed his hand, because she could hear how difficult it had been for him to ask that question. "We have to trust each other," she said quietly. "You get me over the fence before you leave, and you let me do something I am really good at. I'll recon the area, and if everything's all right, I'll find a good place to watch and wait. And if somebody tries to do something they shouldn't, I'll stop them."

The measure of an intelligent man, she thought, is when he allows reason to influence his actions, whether he wants it to or not.

They found a place to leave her car where it couldn't be seen from the road, tucked behind a few yucca trees. Then he changed into his Wyr form. He had a satellite phone as well, but it had been stored at the camp for two cold desert nights, so she brought hers along to be safe. The moon provided some illumination, but the ground was still treacherously uneven, so they jogged at a careful pace for the mile and a half back to his campsite.

He had set camp discreetly among a tumble of large, broken rock, and both site and Jeep were still undisturbed. She started out feeling cold, stiff and tired. Halfway into the run, her muscles loosened and the warm rush of her blood sharpened her thinking.

Once he had agreed to a course of action, Luis didn't waste any time. She walked to keep her muscles warm as he dove into his tent. A few minutes later, he stepped out dressed in jeans, T-shirt, hiking boots and a battered, black leather jacket. He was stuffing something into a pack as he emerged. "Here's a blanket, an MRE and some bottled water," he said. "Should help you stay warm and alert. And I've got a rifle in the Jeep I want you to take."

"You came prepared." Tribunal Peacekeepers were famous for it. They dealt with all kinds of weird shit. She took the pack and handed him the phone, which he tucked into his jacket pocket.

"Standard issue for a field assignment is a rifle, handgun, and a basic camp with three days of meals, especially when there's the possibility of rough terrain," he said. He glanced around. "We're not going to waste time breaking camp. Let's go."

He drove the Jeep the rest of the way. Neither spoke through the increasingly rough ride. A twelve-foot security fence bordered the mine property, but scaling it with the assistance of an oversized Wyr turned out to be no problem. Luis parked the Jeep close to the fence, stood on the hood, threw another blanket over the coiled barbed wire at the top, and hoisted her over as easily as if she weighed forty pounds, not a hundred and forty. She made the drop to the other side, her knees bent for the impact. When she straightened, he tossed the rifle and pack over.

She settled the pack on her back and shouldered the rifle. It was an M16, and she was well familiar with the weapon. Then they stood on opposite sides of the fence, facing each other. Luis nodded to her left. "The gate and office are not quite a mile back. Follow the fence and you can't miss it. There's a guard booth manned by security personnel, but you shouldn't have any trouble avoiding them. It's another quarter mile to the mine entrance. There are a couple of buildings and a parking lot." He regarded her, his face grim, and hooked the fingers of one hand through the fence. "I'm never going to forgive myself if something happens to you."

"Don't fuss," she said. She touched his fingers gently. "The sooner you go, the sooner you'll get back. In the meantime, if we're lucky, nothing will happen here."

He drew in a deep breath and let it out again. It seemed laden with the weight of unsaid words. His hand fell away from the fence. He nodded to her and left.

The wild, silent desert reminded her of Afghanistan. She felt the ghosts of her former companions-in-arms as she hiked the distance back to the mine office and entrance. Losing them hurt, and it was always going to hurt. There would never be any further resolution to what had happened to them, but on that walk, for the first time, she felt a sense of comfort from carrying those ghosts with her, and that was farther than she had ever expected to get.

The area was quiet, the mine offices dark. Luis was right; she didn't have any trouble avoiding security guards. With any luck, they would never know she had been on the property.

A quarter of a mile in, the entrance to the mine was set into a tall, rocky bluff and was surrounded by buildings, a parking lot, and large, darkly shadowed machinery. Recon was quick and easy. She couldn't sense the crossover passage, but that didn't surprise her.

She took a tour of the buildings, and all was quiet, so she decided to go to high ground and find a place to watch and wait. After a careful fifteen-minute climb, she found a ledge wide enough to lie down on, and she rewarded herself by eating the MRE and downing a bottle of water.

Not long after, the sky began to lighten in the east, looking bruised and leaden. It was going to be a dirty dawn, dulled by the aftermath of the storm.

She saw the dust cloud first, and she straightened from her slouch. Two SUVs came into sight, roaring toward her.

Well. That was either good news or bad news. She took the blanket from around her shoulders, folded it and set it aside. Then she stretched out on her stomach, laid the M16 beside her, rested her chin on her hands and watched the arrivals.

It was not good news.

Both SUVs screeched to a halt and six men climbed out. Four men she didn't recognize. Rodriguez. Bradshaw Senior.

Bradshaw had gotten here awfully fast. Too fast. Where had she gone wrong in her calculations? She frowned, her mind racing back.

Then in a flash of realization, it hit. She had estimated travel and response times from the confrontation with Junior and friends. What she should have estimated from was an earlier point in time, when Rodriguez knew that Luis was alive. He would have tried to get in touch with Bradshaw the moment he left Jackson's. Maybe the cell and landlines were out by then. Maybe Rodriguez had to drive the information out. Maybe he had managed to get a call out, but the storm would have grounded any local flights, so Bradshaw would have had to drive in from Vegas.

They wouldn't know Luis was no longer a badly injured, unconscious dog. They probably stopped by Jackson's already and found everybody gone. They might have stopped by Junior's too. Bradshaw might not even know yet what had happened to his son. Either way, he was here to take care of the mine issue himself.

The scene crystallized around her.

She didn't have all the answers, but did she have enough of them? The events of the day passed through her mind. She thought of Luis, of Jackson, of her barroom chat with local people, of what each person had told her and of what she had surmised. She thought of Junior and his friends.

She reached for the rifle and sighted down the barrel.

One shot. One well-timed bullet, aimed at the head of this snake. If she did this, she was putting herself in the line of fire again.

She was not afraid of death. Death was a thief that always wore a mask. Accident, disease, stillbirths, old age, natural causes, war, murder. It existed in the shivering silence between tolls of a bell. It stole everything away while it left its mark, a dark knowledge that lingered at the back of smiling eyes, a hesitation between thought and action in times of danger, a heaviness that tunneled wormholes into happy memories.

She and death had danced together for a long time now. Sometimes they were partners. Sometimes they were opponents. Sometimes she might cheat him, but hell, that old thief was still bound to win some day.

She pulled the trigger.

Chapter Seven

Love

The shot took Bradshaw Senior, who spun backward and collapsed to the ground.

That just left the professionals.

Rodriguez lunged to Bradshaw's motionless figure and dragged him behind the cover of an SUV, while the other four men pulled weapons, shouted to each other and lunged for cover as well. Two started to climb into the drivers' seats.

No, you don't, she thought. *Nobody's leaving until I say so.* She shot out the rear tires of both vehicles, four taps in quick succession.

By then they had her location and returned fire. She ducked, flattening herself as shards of rock ricocheted. Fiery pain bloomed on her back and arms. She ignored it.

The M16 magazine held thirty rounds, and her Glock had fifteen. They had more shooters, more guns, and more rounds. She was going to have to get picky.

She watched and waited as the dirty sky brightened. They tried to flush her out with a heavy rain of bullets. Yeah, that wasn't gonna happen. More ricochets, more nicks. She stayed flattened on her ledge and listened to them expend their resources, and she kept watch, counting her rounds and using them sparingly, just enough to keep them pinned down.

While she did so, she remembered other times when she and death had danced together, the staccato rhythm of heavy artillery, interspersed with anguished screams.

This was a cleaner place. After the first flurry, the targets grew quiet as they tried to think their way out of the invisible cage she put them in. There wasn't a way out, not until she ran out of ammo, and they wouldn't know when that was. Still, somebody had to try to make a run for it. She was ready when he did, the guy sprinting toward the nearest building while the others laid down covering fire.

She dropped him fifteen paces out. It took him a while to crawl back behind the SUV again. None of his buddies rushed out to help. She thought about finishing him as she watched him struggle, weighing the expenditure of another round against reducing their manpower. But one more round was currency that bought her time.

That was her mission, time. She paid for it in snatches when they pushed her to it, and in between bouts of exchanging gunfire, she rested and listened to the wind swept silence.

She had three rounds left when a hurricane arrived. The hurricane materialized into a star-eyed Djinn, Luis and several other tribunal Peacekeepers, and then for Claudia, the dance was over.

✧   ✧   ✧

The aftermath was a hell of a mess.

Over the next few days, correspondents from network, cable and a few foreign newspapers tried to fill up both motels. Several reporters were highly disgruntled when Peacekeeper officials and the FBI, including geologists and crossover experts, commandeered rooms. Then there was a great deal of squawking and flapping until everybody settled into another uneasy pattern, like birds on a wire.

Still other news crews, along with several sightseers, drove RVs in. All the local establishments were doing a booming business, especially the combination truck stop/fast-food joint/casino. Everyone else, the miners and their families, were shocked, grieving and afraid. Most of them hadn't known what was going on and nobody knew whether or not they would have a job in the future. Operations at the Nirvana Silver Mining Company had been halted until further notice.

Sixty-eight undocumented human workers, all foreign nationals, had been recovered from the strange pocket of Other land, along with seven more bodies from shallow graves. The survivors were malnourished, fearful and confused about where they were. Promised work and a new life, they had been driven into the mine at night and taken across the passage to the Other land where they were forced to mine silver for food.

They didn't have any other choice—there were no animals to hunt, nor did the Other land have enough vegetation to support life. The land was literally a buckle in the Earth, little more than magic-sensitive silver, air and rock. The passageway had been buried in a vein of silver and lay inert and undetected until with a few small, controlled blasts, the Nirvana Company had blown it open. The Company blocked the area off and told the legitimate miners the area was unsafe. The passage itself kept the workers captive, since none of them had a spark of Power with which to make the return journey.

Such a lot of fuss over a piece of real estate that was destined by federal law to go unclaimed by anyone.

The downfall of the already wealthy Bradshaw family was greed. Once they uncovered the pocket of Other land and realized what they had found, they had to mine it. They couldn't use the local pool of workers and still hope to keep their activities secret, so they imported workers. As Scott Bradshaw said when he was arrested and questioned in the hospital, one thing led to another.

Bradshaw Senior lived. He was arrested in the hospital too.

When Claudia thought of the seven graves, she wished when she had pulled the trigger that she had made it a kill shot. Instead she'd tagged him high in the shoulder, enough to incapacitate him.

When Luis and the other Peacekeepers arrived, she got to sit back and enjoy watching the take down like prime-time TV. The only thing missing was the popcorn.

Good Christ, did Luis have moves. He was all power and grace, and sex-savvy smarts. She watched him with an odd kind of pained pride. She recognized talent when she saw it, and his star was definitely on the rise. He was the total package. It wouldn't be long before he held a Senior Peacekeeper position.

Even as he chased Rodriguez down and pinned him to the pavement, Luis raised his head and searched for her. She lifted a hand and waggled her fingers. Soon as he caught sight of her, he left Rodriguez handcuffed and spread-eagled on the ground and raced toward her, climbing up to her ledge with athletic effortlessness.

He went into a frenzy when he discovered she had taken damage from chips of rock that had ricocheted during the firefight. She hadn't slept since early the previous morning, and she was too tired to fend off his fussing, so she let him do what he wanted. He bandaged three deep cuts and several nicks then he ran his hands gently down her body, dark eyes sharp with concern as he checked for further wounds.

All right, who was she kidding, she might have enjoyed that a little bit too. She didn't even need to climb down off the ledge. Luis got his Djinn buddy to give her a ride. All in all, it was a cushy wrap-up.

He insisted she get medical treatment, and an EMT suggested stitches. Then Luis scared up a healing potion from somewhere. She never did find out from where. He would not stop harping at her until she drank it. Then more enforcement people arrived and there were the inevitable questions, a whole shitload of them.

She asked for coffee and got it, and she savored the hot caffeine as she answered the questions patiently. For the most part, Luis wasn't present because he had his own job to do and people to answer to. But it just so happened that he was present for her full explanation of the bar confrontation, and his earlier frenzy was nothing compared to the rage that detonated in his body then.

She could feel it pouring off him in deadly waves as he sat beside her, until she couldn't stand it. She gripped his forearm hard until she drew his attention, and she recognized Junior's death blazing in Luis's eyes.

She just looked at the whole great, clenched length of that splendid man, and she gave him a small smile, and she wouldn't let go until he calmed. It took a while, and that was okay. For him, she had discovered she had all the time in the world, if only he knew it.

Then all at once the tension in his body uncoiled. He blew out a breath, covered her hand with his and let it go, and somehow it all combined to make her fall into the most impossible, complete and inappropriate love with him.

The realization was gorgeous, hellish. She drew back and felt more wounded than she had ever felt in her life. She could tell he sensed something serious was wrong, but it wasn't an acceptable topic for discussion, so she did the only thing she knew to do. She went deep into herself, into silence.

Claudia. Was. Driving. Luis. Bat shit.

She'd dealt with the chaos at the mine entrance with the poise of an accomplished professional, answered the barrage of questions with dignity and tolerance, and she'd reacted to the news from the mine with compassion. He thought he might be able to gaze at her for the rest of his life and learn something about intelligent decency in the face of adversity.

The more he watched her, the more he couldn't look away.

He stopped noticing other women. Once, when he paid to gas up the Jeep, it was only when he saw disappointment droop the pretty cashier's shoulders that he realized, belatedly, that the woman had been trying to flirt with him.

But something had happened. Something had caused Claudia to stop speaking to him.

Oh, she *spoke* to him. She wasn't rude, and she didn't subject him to total silence. But something essential had shifted. A wall had come between them, and he could even pinpoint when the change had occurred.

She had been looking right at him. He'd seen her eyes widen as if she'd been struck a blow. Then her expression smoothed over, and she'd started to treat him with the same competent fucking professionalism as she treated everyone else.

Before, they'd shared a connection. It was open, caring and vital, and it mattered to him. He didn't think it had just vanished. She'd buried it for some reason. He'd waited for a while because he kept expecting it to change back, that the connection would return to the surface, but it hadn't. And then he'd grown pissed at her for taking that away from him.

After the mine shut down, the days progressed. Luis had a long talk with his grandmother. He promised to visit her soon, but for the moment he had work to do.

There was always cleanup after a case, and this one was particularly messy. Jackson returned from Fresno. Claudia stayed in the back trailer, and Luis took one of Jackson's spare bedrooms. Luis told himself he took Jackson's invitation because he didn't feel like sharing a motel room with another Peacekeeper, but really, he knew better.

Raoul, the Peacekeeper Djinn, found a nine-hole golf course just west of town. The Djinn loved any kind of sport, and so did Luis. After work one evening, in an effort to blow off steam, he went with Raoul to thwack a golf ball around the course a couple of times. The layout of the holes was basic, and the course wasn't very well maintained, so they soon lost interest and went drinking instead.

Claudia honored the "don't go anywhere" admonition she'd been given. She spent a lot of time quietly reading and avoiding reporters. More often than not, she, Jackson and Luis ate dinner together, their conversations dominated by the latest discovery from the mine. Since they were all indifferent cooks, they took turns picking up takeout from the diner.

By the third day, Luis'd had it.

There was no drama, no explosion. He just got tired of waiting for things to change, so he went on the offensive. It felt good to finally follow his instincts, to stop throttling back, and, he had to be honest, it felt good to be challenged.

He started out small, stalking Claudia in subtle ways over the next few days. When they stood talking, he got a bit too close, invading her space. At the dinner table, when she passed the salt to him, he reached a little too far for it, closing his hand over hers. He slid his fingers down the length of her hand until he could grasp the shaker. Her bland expression didn't change, but her pupils dilated, and sudden arousal thrummed low, rhythmic notes in her scent.

And there it was again, the connection.

He was clever enough not to show his triumph.

She liked to go running early. On the seventh morning, she emerged from the trailer, dressed in running clothes with her pale hair pulled back.

He was waiting for her in his Wyr form. She jerked to a halt when she saw him sitting in the yard, and this time she looked shaken. He didn't wag his tail. He just waited for her to make up her mind.

She came slowly down the steps. "Oh, Precious," she said. For some reason she sounded sad. For the first time in days she touched him voluntarily, laying a gentle hand on his head. Everything inside of him concentrated on the sensation of the warm, light weight of her palm resting on him. Deeper and more profound than pleasure, he felt comfort and recognition. She rubbed one of his ears before her hand fell away.

When he stood, his shoulders came up to her waist. She turned and started to run. He flowed along the ground beside her, his powerful body moving effortlessly, and for a while they shared perfect, seamless movement. The colors of the morning were so pure and new, they were downright righteous, and the air was biting cold. He could have run forever with her like that, but of course it had to end as the obligations of the day took over.

Later, when he let himself into Jackson's house, around five, Luis found a note. Jackson had been called away on a vet emergency. They should eat dinner without him.

Luis thought about that. It was Claudia's turn to get takeout. He went out the back, knocked on the trailer door and a moment later she opened it. The westering sun caught her full in the face, shining on her sleek, shoulder-length pale hair and turning her green eyes emerald. She was wearing jeans and a T-shirt, and it was so goddamn erotic to see how that shirt molded to her tight, lean torso. His gaze fell down her length.

She was barefoot.

Suddenly he was rock hard with agonized hunger.

He looked up again and smiled. "Pick up meat loaf dinners for me and Jackson?"

"Sure," she said. She glanced past him at the empty space where Jackson parked his truck. "I didn't realize it had gotten so late. Where's Dan?"

"He'll be back," Luis said.

She nodded. "Give me half an hour."

"You bet."

He went back to the house to take a quick shower, putting on jeans and a T-shirt too. Then he let himself into the trailer to wait for her. He stopped dead just inside the door.

After a week, her possessions had gradually taken over the trailer until evidence of her stay was everywhere. Not that she was untidy; she was very neat. But there were books, movies she borrowed from Jackson's collection, her suitcase, the laptop, phone and charger, the Tarot deck.

Until now. Everything was packed, and she had cleaned. The laptop was stored in its case, and an open canvas bag held her paperbacks and phone, and the Tarot deck sat neatly on top.

Man, she was slamming that wall into place again with a vengeance.

Emotion roared through him, a gigantic, silent outcry that gnawed at his bones like acid. *Oh, no you don't*, he said to the emptiness.

No, you don't.

Claudia stepped into the trailer, carrying three Styrofoam containers and a paper bag full of the requisite dinner rolls, and it was her turn to stop dead just inside the door.

Violence lounged on the end of the sofa, and it looked a lot like Luis. He was playing with the Tarot deck, his big, brown hands dexterous as he handled the cards.

She took in his set expression and blazing eyes. Yeah, she wasn't going to go anywhere near that. She stepped away, into the miniscule kitchen area. "Where's Dan?"

"Vet emergency."

She set the dinners on the counter, listening to him shuffle the deck. *Snap. Snap. Snap.* She looked at the table. He was snapping each card as he laid them down in what looked like a basic spread, but he clearly wasn't paying attention to what he was doing.

She said, "You knew Dan was out on the emergency before, didn't you?"

His sensual mouth drew tight. "Yep."

Dinner lost its appeal. She turned and leaned back against the kitchen sink. "I'm leaving in the morning."

"I got that when I came inside and found your bags packed." He slapped the rest of the deck down, stood and walked toward her. He still hadn't found time to get his hair cut, and the ends of it flopped in his eyes. The angry heat in his expression blinded her to everything else.

"Don't crowd me," she said as he came close. He didn't listen but he also didn't touch her. It was a damn fine line between what was too close and what was too much, and he walked that line well. He braced his hands on the overhead cabinets on either side of her, the heavy muscles of his triceps bunching as he leaned his weight on his arms and looked at her.

She could control her actions but she couldn't control her reaction to him. He pulled it from her, until she felt it flaring from her skin like a fever.

He said softly, "We have a topic of conversation we shelved a while back."

"We don't have anything to talk about," she said. She forced herself to breathe evenly. "I'm a forty-year-old human woman, and you're what—a twenty-five-year-old Wyr?"

"Twenty-seven."

Her eyebrows quirked, mocking the difference. "Twenty-seven," she said. "You have your whole life ahead of you, and it's going to be a hell of a lot longer than a human one. While I am not ever going to be any better than what I am right now, and what I am right now isn't going to last very long. You're starting your career. I just ended one. We are perfectly mismatched."

"Then why do we fit so well?" he whispered.

"We don't." She glared, suddenly as angry with him as she had ever been with anyone. She would never have children. She might have twenty more years left, or she might have forty, and all of those years would be spent aging. She would be dead before she saw any similar signs of aging in a Wyr of his years. "And I do not go for younger men."

"Try convincing your body of that," he said. He leaned forward and kissed her.

And kissed her. And he was too goddamn clever for his own good, because if he had been diffident and had pulled back, she could have regained some ground. As it was, all the blood in her body was pounding so loudly she couldn't think, she could only feel that generous, sensual, optimistic mouth of his moving on hers with a kind of pleading hunger he had not let himself verbalize.

He kissed her like he was starving. He kissed her like she was the first woman he had ever kissed, and heh, well, she knew that couldn't be true, but it was a fine,

fine fairy tale, and good Christ, it was irresistibly seductive. Before she could stop herself, her mouth was moving in response to his.

Angry. She was angry at him. At something. Falling in love with this incredible man hurt like a heart attack. She grabbed his thick, too-long hair and yanked it. His hands came down from the cupboard. He snatched her against him, and the pleading hunger that his gorgeous, sensitive lips communicated so eloquently became a ravening need. A sound came out of him when his tongue stroked along hers, something between a groan and a whine, and his big body started to shake.

He said her name against her lips then he pulled back just far enough so that she could see how the passion darkened his skin and brought a breakable expression into his eyes.

Suddenly her own hurt vanished, and she realized the extent of her own foolishness. The *only* and *forever*, and *falling in love*—that was all in her mind. He didn't need to know the full story of what she felt. She was robbing herself of a rare, wonderful opportunity tonight if she denied this, and him.

"It's okay, Luis," she whispered. She put her arms around his neck and held him tight. "It's all right."

He was burning up. He ran his huge, flattened hands down the gentle curve of her back, and he gripped her hips. She was surprised when he pulled away. Then realization lanced into her as he knelt, lifted the hem of her t-shirt and teased open the fastening of her jeans.

"Jesus," she said as he kissed her flat, tight stomach.

"I've been wanting to do this for days. And days. And days." His breath blasted the tiny hairs on her sensitive skin, and she listed drunkenly against the counter. He eased her shoes and socks off, then yanked her jeans down to her ankles, breathing hard. Then her underwear, until the pale, silken tangle of her pubic hair was bared. She had a scar on her hip, one of the times she got grazed by enemy fire. His trembling fingers traced the path of the mark on her skin. He breathed, "Hook your leg over my shoulder."

She hissed a curse, because now he made her shake all over too. At his coaxing, she balanced her weight on one wobbly leg while he lifted the other leg and draped it over one broad shoulder. She watched him stare at the most private part of her that was hypersensitive with arousal, and then he looked up at her taut, incredulous face.

Then he heaved a sigh as heartfelt as if he was coming home. He leaned into her and gently, avidly took her clitoris in his mouth, and there was no playing the fiction that this was his first time for that, because he knew just what the fuck he was doing, and he did it superlatively.

"I'm dying here," she groaned. He made a soothing sound at the back of his throat while he licked, nibbled and suckled. Raw jolts of pleasure rocked through her, and if she hadn't been gripping the edge of the kitchen sink or clutching his hair, she would have fallen.

His fingers probed gently at the slick entrance to her vagina while his mouth worked her. She pushed her hips against him, sobbing for breath. She was dying, he was killing her, killing her. The sensations were too intense, too sharp. She had been partnerless for too long. She had grown too accustomed to bringing her own release. He was never going to get her to come.

But then he did. The climax seared through her nerve endings and tore a sound of delirious pleasure from her.

He pulled away slowly and leaned his forehead against the curve of her pubic bone, breathing as though he was at a full-out run. Unclenching her fist from his hair, she stroked the side of his face while he gripped her hips, calloused fingers rubbing along her skin.

She lifted the leg that had been draped along his back, put her bare foot to his collarbone, and kicked him back so that he sprawled on the floor. As he went down, she came on top of him, straddling his hips, and he opened his mouth, that fabulously sensual, wickedly clever mouth still slick with her pleasure, and before he could say anything, she dove down to kiss him hard.

He muttered something guttural and flexed his hips as he grabbed her by the back of the neck, and this time they didn't kiss so much as eat at each other's mouths, rough with an escalating urgency that spread like a wildfire. Time burned away. They both felt for the fastening of his jeans, trying to help each other and tangling their fingers. When the fastening finally came undone, he yanked the zipper down and she closed her fingers over his erection.

Hell's bells, he was a big sonovabitch there too. He really was going to kill her. She eased up so that she could look down the rippling contours of his long, muscled torso. His penis was as beautiful as the rest of him, with a velvet-soft, broad head, and a thick, hard length.

"Ooh, Precious," she said, looking up at him with a quick grin, and sudden laughter creased his face. Then his laughter vaporized as she stroked him, all the way down to his balls which had drawn up tight, and he shuddered all over.

She guided him to her entrance. He stopped her, hands shaking. "Condom?"

She shook her head and whispered, "No need." She had used an IUD until her mid-thirties. Once she was sure she wasn't cut out to parent a child, she'd settled the issue permanently with surgery.

When his resistance vanished, she eased down on him. She had a thought that she ought to warn him to take this part slow, since those were the only muscles in her body that she hadn't exercised in a while. But he was so gentle as he pushed up, while his expression was so drawn with need, she went a little crazy and impaled herself on him in one painful, glorious movement.

Then he was seated in her all the way, and they stared at each other. The slanting evening sunshine spilled in through a nearby window and fell over them in a rain of gold. He pulled on her t-shirt and she sat straight up to drag it over her head, and to remove her bra too. His gaze was wide, wondering. Her breasts weren't very big, and she didn't think they were interesting, but he touched them with a reverence that made her eyes moisten.

I love you, she told him silently. You impossibly wonderful man.

Because she could say whatever she wanted in her own head. Because she could confess it all, as he began to flex underneath her, moving gently. He stroked her breast, stroked her face, and then their bodies came together just right, and she arched her back as she peaked again. Her pleasure must have hurtled him forward, because he gripped her by the hips again, hard, pumping up once, twice, and then he groaned and climaxed along with her.

She fell forward, sprawling on him, and fought to get control of her breathing. His arms closed around her, and there was nothing more perfect than the moment when he was still inside her and he held her so tightly. He whispered her name.

They hadn't even gotten his shirt or his jeans off. Man, she really knew how to trash herself. She pressed a kiss to his hot, damp neck and thought, *I'm a goddamn idiot.*

Luis rolled her over and made love to her again. And again.

Here was the fun bit: clearly she hadn't had a Wyr lover before, because she was all wide-eyed astonishment at his stamina, and she didn't connect to the significance of his multiple orgasms.

That last time, they had managed to get to their feet. The sun had set but the light was not fully gone, and he'd finally kicked off the last of his clothes. He swiped the cards out of the way, bent her over the table and took her from behind.

He knew she was wrecked, exhausted. He had wrung every climax he could out of her, so that last time was pure, greedy selfishness on his part, an orgiastic wallow in her magnificent, athletic body. She just laughed as he plunged urgently into her. She reached behind, gripped him by the back of his neck and held on as he bit her shoulder, growled and twisted up in one final, exquisite spasm.

Afterward, he stood at the counter, still nude, and ate a lukewarm dinner, while she sat at the table and collected the scattered cards with slow, tired movements. She had grabbed a blanket from the bed and wrapped it around her torso. Her hair was tangled and she had bite marks down her neck.

He stared at the marks he had made. He'd really gone to town, marking her, and she had egged him on. She had marked him too, and he had loved her ferocity. It was the only time he had ever been frustrated with his own rapid healing, because he wanted to wear every single scratch she had given him.

Gods, he couldn't wait until they made love again. When Wyr mated, they did so for life, and the mating period was a bit frenzied for a couple of months.

She haphazardly stacked the cards together and set the deck aside.

"I don't know if I got them all," she said, her voice blurred with tiredness. "I don't think I can count right now."

"We can check later." He put the other two meals in the fridge.

She put her head in her hands. "Luis, I'm still leaving in the morning."

He walked over to the table as he thought of how to answer. "I know. Let's go to bed."

He happened to glance down at the Tarot deck as he spoke. Inanna, the goddess of Love, lay at the top of the deck. The hand painted card was quite stunning, actually. Inanna was a golden woman, and seven lions pulled her chariot.

He tapped the card. Yeah, there was a reason why the goddess was so fierce and surrounded by lions. Sometimes love was a dance, and maybe sometimes, for some people, it was hearts and flowers.

Occasionally it was an all-or-nothing battle.

He figured things might get downright tricky for a little while. He didn't need the message from the Tarot spread he had laid out earlier; he already knew he was at a crossroads.

He still had time. He could pull away from Claudia. He didn't have to mate irrevocably with her.

But if there was anyone in this wide, wicked world who deserved the kind of devotion he had to give, it was her. He might have to leverage and scheme, but he would do his goddamn best to convince her of that. And well, damn it, once you started walking a warrior's path, you pretty much had to accept that you ran the risk of living a short life.

They would burn each other up. They would burn too fast. But they would burn brightly.

You gonna help me out any here? he asked the goddess. He supposed it was a prayer of sorts. Inanna smiled out of the card and said nothing.

He followed Claudia to the bed alcove and curled his body around hers. She turned her face into his shoulder and fell asleep immediately, while he held her for the rest of the night.

Things were going to get interesting in the morning.

Early the next morning, Luis left.

"Good-bye," Claudia said gently when she kissed him.

His expression set, he returned her kiss, hard, and said nothing.

She refused to let that hurt her feelings. Once Luis was gone, she ate part of her meat loaf dinner for breakfast and threw the rest away. Then she straightened the trailer one last time. She did count the cards in the Tarot deck to make sure she'd found them all. On impulse, she shuffled them and flipped over the first seven. Not a single one of the Major Arcana showed up.

Somehow that didn't surprise her. She stacked the cards in their box, threw the box in the bag on top of the paperbacks again, and set the bag in her back seat. Much later, she distinctly remembered that, when she looked for the deck in every nook and cranny of the car but couldn't find it.

When she was done packing up the car, she went to hug Jackson good-bye. He gave her a rib bruising in return. "You better not disappear for good," he said.

"I'll call you next week," she said. "And I'll come back to visit late summer."

He sucked a tooth and grumbled. "That's all right, then."

As she pulled away from the house, her heart emptied until she felt hollow and light as air.

A dusty Jeep pulled up behind her as she drove down the street, and when she saw it in her rearview mirror, suddenly she was full up again and twisted with riotous emotion.

Damn it, what was Luis up to?

He followed her sedately through town. The Jeep turned into a parking space at the gas station/fast-food joint/casino, while she pulled up to a pump.

Her jaw angled out. She decided to ignore him, as she went about the business of filling up her gas tank.

A full Greyhound bus pulled into the parking lot. She gritted her teeth and watched with resignation as the occupants disembarked and headed indoors. There were several small family units, a few retirees, a couple of Light Fae teenagers, and a young medusa wearing goth makeup, with her short, slim head snakes wrapped for travel.

So much for short lines and a quick getaway. Claudia wasn't about to head into the desert without at least a couple bottles of water in the car, even if she was traveling on a major highway. After filling her tank, she sucked it up and went inside to the Food Mart.

Eventually she made her way outside again, having acquired half a dozen bottles of water and a shortened temper.

She found Luis lounging against the wall in the sunshine, a duffle bag at his feet. He wore scuffed boots, faded jeans, a gray t-shirt, his black leather jacket and a scowl. She looked at his strong, graceful neck, where his satin-brown skin disappeared under his shirt, and she wanted to bite him again, to claw at that perfection while she took him into her body. Surely the gods had not been fair when they'd made that man so damn beautiful.

She dragged her gaze away and squinted at the early morning sun. "What are you doing here, Precious?"

Luis said, "I'm not done having sex with you yet."

It took a split second for that to sink in. She spun on her heel, spoiling for a fight.

He gave her a slow smile that was both remarkably sweet and naughty at the same time. His grandmother must have warned him that smile might land him in jail or at the wrong end of a shotgun at a wedding.

Her expression compressed. Then the edge of her mouth took on a slight, unwilling tilt. "I spent most of my adult life in the army. You think you can shock me with that kind of shit?"

His smile widened. He stepped close and ran the tip of his finger lightly down her cheek. "I got time off for good behavior, and injuries incurred on the job. I was coming back to the house to tell you, but you were already taking off. I've called someone to come pick up the Jeep. I don't have to be back at work for at least another month, maybe even six weeks if I sound pathetic enough over the phone. I figure that means I get to hang out with you for a while."

Doubts crowded in. She felt uncharacteristically torn between what she wanted so badly and what her mind told her was the right path to take. "This is a terrible idea."

He gave her an exasperated look. "Did I ask you what you thought?"

She bit the inside of her cheek. She couldn't make herself tell him to go away. It wasn't right to tell him he could come. She turned and stalked back to her car. He had gotten her so rattled, she had forgotten to lock her doors, and she never forgot to lock her doors. As she threw the bottled water in the back and climbed into the car, he set his duffle bag in the back seat and angled his long body into the passenger's side.

Claudia slapped her hands on the steering wheel. "Luis."

He settled back, the picture of contentment. "Shut up and drive."

✧   ✧   ✧

OTHER WORKS BY THEA HARRISON

Dragos Takes a Holiday
Divine Tarot (Print Ed. True Colors & Natural Evil)
Destiny's Tarot (Print Ed. Devil's Gate & Hunter's
Season)